PH(

DAWN SULLIVAN

Dedication

To my husband and family for all of their love and support. Without them, I would not be where I am today.

Chapter 1

Shudders racked her body. The pain in her chest was excruciating. Where was she? What had happened? Serenity could not remember. Wait...she had been shot. That's right. No, she was not the one that was shot. Another woman had been shot. There had been a rescue attempt at the facility where Serenity and several other women were being held by a psychopath known only as the General. He had started a breeding program pairing men and women with various psychic abilities, many of which were also shifters. The reason for his fascination with the program was unknown to others. The General had several facilities where he held the women. The largest one was where Serenity had been. He kept the women in the larger facility until they were pregnant and then moved them to a smaller facility until after the children were born. During the chaos of the attempt to free the women, Serenity was once again captured by the General after a guard had previously knocked her out with a drug making her defenseless. Not only had Serenity been taken, but the other woman had been shot and captured as well. Serenity had helped her by using her healing gift to mend the broken flesh made by the bullet wound, and taking away her pain. Unfortunately, Serenity had failed to fully heal her. She had not been strong enough with the drugs that the guard had given her still in her system. Now she was paying for what she had done. This was why she resisted the urge to use her abilities most of the time. When Serenity healed, she took the pain from the other person and it became her pain. It left her weak and vulnerable, and she was unable to protect herself. But the woman had been in so much pain, and Serenity had not been able to resist helping her. She had been human and might not have made it if Serenity had not healed her and provided relief from her suffering.

Serenity had avoided using her healing abilities since being captured by the General. She had been hiding it from him. He thought she was just a wolf shifter, and Serenity had been happy to let him think that. The General also did not realize that she was telepathic. As far as he had known, she did not possess psychic abilities. Serenity would not have been able to stay out of the breeding program for as long as she had if he had known the extent of her gifts. And Serenity would do anything to get away from being groped, pawed and fucked by every man around. The General used her more as an experiment than anything else. The scientists took her blood, among other things, and she let them. It was better than the alternative.

Shudders continued to rack Serenity's body as she struggled to remember everything that had happened. It was all so foggy in her mind. As she lay there in pain, she tried to figure out what the hell was going on.

Phoenix. She remembered Phoenix. Ashley, one of the other women being held with her, had told her about a vision she'd had. Phoenix was Serenity's mate, and he was coming for her. Wait, he had come for her, but he wasn't there now. That's right, the General had taken her. Oh God, the General still had her. Phoenix, where was Phoenix? She needed him. She was so scared. She was defenseless right now, and she knew it. With Phoenix the last thought in her mind, she passed out again.

The next time when Serenity came to, the pain was bearable. It still hurt, but it was slowly ebbing away. This she could handle. Serenity knew if she shifted once she would heal even faster, but she refused to shift in front of any of the guards or scientists, and especially not in front of the General. First of all, she would have to take off her clothes to shift or they would be shredded. But more importantly, the General loved to watch them shift and she refused to give him the satisfaction of seeing what she looked like in wolf form. She had taken several beatings over her refusal, but it was worth it to piss the General off. The only time she had ever allowed her wolf to come out was late at night when everyone else was asleep. The video cameras in her room would somehow malfunction a couple of times a month, thanks to one of the scientists in the facility, and she would allow herself to spend a few hours in her wolf form.

"Why did you do it?" she heard a voice say. "I could have handled it. You shouldn't have taken the pain from me. I would have been fine. Why did you do it?"

Serenity slowly opened her eyes and looked at the woman staring down at her. "For Phoenix," she whispered weakly. "I did it for Phoenix." As the other woman's dark brown eyes widened in surprise, Serenity slipped into a deep healing sleep.

Chapter 2

It had been four days. Four fucking days, and they still had no leads on where Serenity and Rikki were being held. Both his mate and his sister had been kidnapped. That bastard, the General, had them. Phoenix sat in a chair on Angel's back porch with his elbows on his knees holding his head in his hands. All he could think about was Serenity and Rikki and how he had failed them. If only he could have saved them

Phoenix was part of an elite mercenary group that went by the name of RARE; Rescue and Retrieval Extractions. They were a team of six lead by Angel Johnston. RARE found out the General was holding women with the intention of breeding them for their shifter and psychic abilities. For what purpose, they still had no idea. Jaxson, RARE's resident electronics expert, was working on the puzzle night and day, hacking into any site he could find that might have some answers. But there were none. All the team knew, at this time, was the General was a sick bastard who got off on hurting innocent women.

Gathered intel showed there had been one large facility in the Shenandoah Mountains and several smaller ones in various locations where women and children were being held. While RARE hit the larger one, the shifter council sent a number of their enforcers to hit the smaller ones with the help of the area shifter communities. Unfortunately, the General had found out RARE's plan of attack, and he moved several of the facilities before the attacks could take place. The council enforcers were only able to take down four of the smaller facilities. The General had also moved all but nine women out of the biggest facility.

In the end, it had been a huge cluster fuck. Seven women were saved but two were still missing. One was Rikki, a member of RARE. She had given up her freedom, and possibly her life, so Nico could go home to his mate, Jenna and child, Lily.

The other was Serenity, who Phoenix later found out from one the women that were held in the larger facility, was his mate. After having a premonition, one of the women had told Serenity about Phoenix and that he was coming for her. Before RARE had made it to the facility, a guard had tried to force himself on Serenity. She had fought him, slicing his chest open with her claws. The guard had beaten her, drugged her and had thrown her in a room by herself. When the General left the building, he'd grabbed Serenity and ran, using her as a shield to get to a waiting helicopter. At the time, Phoenix had been so hell bent on saving Nico that he had not paid much attention to the woman with the General. He had just gotten a glimpse of a tiny woman with long dark hair. Since hearing Serenity was his mate, Phoenix wished he had paid more attention.

God, all Phoenix had wanted was to find that special someone, a woman who would complete him. He wanted someone who would always be there for him, no matter what. Phoenix was so tired of the fast hookups that were going nowhere. He was lonely, so damn lonely for so long. Then when Nico and Jenna found each other, he discovered that when shifters mated, it was like merging their souls together. Once they found each other, they would always be together and would never stray. He wanted that for himself. Phoenix was human, but he knew shifters mated with humans, too. He had also known chances were slim that there was a mate for him, but he had been holding out, praying he would get lucky enough to find out what being mated to a shifter was like.

Well, he was finding out it was pure hell. Serenity was out there. That psychotic bastard had her, and who knew what was happening to her now? Serenity, his mate. Phoenix was going to find her. He was going to save her. Then he was going to hunt down every last motherfucker that had hurt her and make them pay because she was his, and nobody touched what was his.

Chapter 3

Angel cursed as her phone rang once again. She did not have time for this. She was not taking on any other missions until she brought Rikki and Serenity home. Jeremiah Black, a man that RARE contracted jobs with, had been trying to get a hold of her for the last 24 hours. Angel knew she needed to talk to him, but she refused to answer the phone or even listen to the messages yet. Someone obviously needed rescued, but as far as Angel was concerned, that was not her problem. Her family was her number one priority. Right now the only thing she worried about was finding out where the General was hiding Rikki and Serenity.

As her phone went to voice mail, she looked up at Jaxson and asked, "What do you have? Anything?"

"Nothing. I've gone through everything we got from the computers in that last facility, and there's nothing here. Not a damn thing! I can't find any other locations where that bastard is holding women. We have hit them all. I have no clue where the new facilities are. I have nothing," Jaxson growled in frustration, raking a hand through his short blond hair.

Angel had been trying to connect telepathically with Rikki, but she had not been successful...yet. It didn't feel like Rikki was gone, Angel just could not connect to her. Rikki could be drugged or unconscious. Unfortunately, there was no way of knowing what the real reason was.

Just then, Phoenix came through the door. "Tell me ya got something, Angel," he demanded.

"Nothing," Angel said. "Nothing. I can't connect with Rikki. I tried again this morning. For some reason, I just can't. It is like there's a block."

"What about Serenity?" Trace, one of RARE's team members, asked. "Can you connect with her?"

"I doubt it," Angel said. "I only saw her the one time. I would need something of hers like a piece of clothing. Without anything, there's no way."

"Please, try," Phoenix said. "Please, for me." Angel looked over at Phoenix and the pain in his eyes. She could not imagine what he was going through right now. To Angel, Rikki was like family; but Phoenix had not only lost Rikki, whom he had loved like a sister, but he had lost his mate too. She just could not imagine it. "Yeah, Phoenix," Angel sighed, "Yeah, I'll try."

"Nico," she called out. "Get a hold of Jenna and see if she can talk to the women who were at the facility with Serenity. See if they have anything, anything at all, that belonged to Serenity. Hell, anything she even touched might help. Get me something that will help me connect with her."

"I'm on it," Nico said as he grabbed his cell phone and walked over to a quiet corner of the conference room.

"I know it's a long shot, but thank you for trying, Angel," Phoenix said. Angel nodded, as she pulled out her cell phone to listen to Jeremiah's messages. He needed an extraction of course. Unfortunately for him, RARE was not available. Since it was the third message he had left, she decided she had better call him back.

Chapter 4

Jeremiah Black tugged on his tie and then adjusted the collar of his white button down shirt. He hated dressing up. He hated the bureaucratic bullshit of his job. He was tired of manipulating everyone and everything in the system to get things done. But where else could he track down bad guys and make them face justice the way that he did for the FBI? Fuck, he was just trying to save lives.

Yeah, he was tired of it. He was tired of a lot of things. Most of all, he was tired of staying away from his mate. His sexy, gorgeous, tough as hell mate. Jeremiah had met her just over a year ago, but he had not allowed himself to follow through on the mate bond, not yet. His mate seemed so young, and he could tell that she had ghosts in her past. She had not been ready for him, and she definitely had not been ready for his bear. So, he had decided to wait. But he could not fight the bond any longer. No, Jeremiah refused to fight the bond any longer.

The funny thing was, she had no idea that Jeremiah was her mate. She was human, and while shifters instantly recognized their mates, humans were slower to acknowledge the bond. She would feel a pull towards him, but probably did not know why. Chances were she thought it was just attraction, and if that were the case, there was no way in hell she would ever act on it.

Jeremiah had met his mate the first time RARE had contracted a mission for the FBI. After he realized who she was, he had delved in her background. Jeremiah found out that she had grown up in foster care. She had constantly been moved to different homes until she had run away at age 15. She lived on the streets until she enlisted in the army at age 18. She had served two terms, becoming one of the best snipers the army had ever seen. After an honorable discharge from the Army, his mate joined Angel's team. That was two years ago. She lived a life of danger now, and he knew without question, she would continue to work with Angel even after she and Jeremiah bonded. The question was, how was he going to get her to recognize their bond? She was so damn stubborn, but Jeremiah liked that about her. He liked, no loved, so many things about her; he loved her loyalty to her team, her courageousness, her expressive dark brown eyes, her beautiful long brown hair, her plump fuck me lips that he wanted wrapped around his dick. Jeremiah groaned softly.

Yeah, the next time Jeremiah saw her, he was not going to be able to hold himself back. He didn't want to, and neither did his bear. He could not wait to see her again. Just then his desk phone rang. "Black here," he barked into the receiver.

"Jeremiah, it's Angel. Sorry I haven't answered your calls."

"It's alright, Angel. I got a job for RARE."

"I'm not taking any jobs, Jeremiah. Not now, not for a while."

What? What the hell was she talking about? "I need ya on this one, Angel. A well-known government official was kidnapped two days ago and we haven't been able to locate him."

"I can't do it, Jeremiah. I'm sorry, but I have to pass. One of my team members has been taken. Until I get her back, no jobs."

Jeremiah froze. "Taken?" he ground out through clenched teeth. "Who?"

"Rikki," Angel whispered. "Son of a bitch got her. We couldn't get to her in time. We have been trying to hunt her down, Jeremiah, but we haven't been able to find her."

"What the fuck," he roared. "Talk to me, Angel. Tell me what's going on with my mate!" Ah shit. He hadn't meant to acknowledge to anyone Rikki was his mate. Especially since Rikki didn't know.

"Your what?" Angel asked in shock. "My mate," he growled. "Rikki is mine. You tell me what the fuck is going on."

Angel just sat there. "She's yours? Why didn't you say anything?"

"She wasn't ready. Where is she? Who has her?" Jeremiah growled, trying to get his bear under control as his fangs threatened to drop.

"You better come to my house. The team and I will tell you everything. It's not good though, Jeremiah," Angel whispered. "It's not good."

Jeremiah replaced the receiver, and immediately picked it up again, calling to have the plane ready for takeoff as soon as possible. He was going to get his mate back. No one was taking her from him. And when he got her back, he was not letting her go.

Jeremiah got up and walked out of his office. "I'm leaving," he told his agent, Cord. "I'm not sure how long I will be gone. You're in charge for now."

"What are you talking about?" Cord asked. "You can't leave. We have this huge case on the verge of exploding and.."

"Yeah, well I have something more important to take care of," Jeremiah interrupted. "I'm leaving. The big boss man can fire me if he wants, but I'm outta here."

"Where are you going?" Cord asked in confusion. "To save my woman," Jeremiah growled as he slammed out of the office.

Jeremiah went straight home, loaded up one duffle bag with clothes and another with various weapons and supplies he might need to rescue his mate. He may have been an office boy for a while now, but he still knew how to kick ass. He was going to join RARE on this one whether they wanted him to or not. Rikki was his, dammit, his.

Chapter 5

"What's going on?" Nico asked as Angel hung up her cell phone, slowly sitting it down on the table.

"Well isn't that craptastick?" she whispered, her big blue eyes wide with surprise. "What?" Nico asked. "Jeremiah Black is Rikki's mate," Angel said as she sat there letting it all sink in.

"Oh shit," Jaxson said. They all knew Jeremiah Black. Good man. Bear shifter. Tough as nails. He was going to come in guns blazing. But Angel was thrilled. She needed him. She would have asked for his help before, but she hadn't been sure she would get it. He worked for the FBI. He was under their rules and regulations. RARE did not answer to anyone. They *did not* answer to the FBI, the CIA, not even Homeland Security. RARE did its own thing. They contracted work out to several different agencies, but they handled things their way, with no questions asked. As long as the job got done, everyone was happy. Jeremiah Black worked for the FBI, but he was a badass bear shifter. All bets were off now. Someone had taken his mate, and Angel knew he would do whatever it took to get her back. She was glad he was on their side.

Just then, Nico's phone rang. He answered, listened for a few minutes, and said, "See ya as soon as you can get here."

Turning towards Phoenix he said, "We are in luck, my brother. A couple of weeks ago a new girl, Summer, showed up at the facility. She was really young and scared to death. Becca, a scientist that worked there, snuck her into Serenity's room the first night to comfort her. Serenity had a necklace that she had been wearing when the General's men stole her from her pack. For some reason, they let her keep it. She gave it to Summer that first night and told her it would help keep her safe. Chase is getting the necklace and bringing it here."

Phoenix did not want to get his hopes up, but this was their best bet so far. If Angel could connect with Serenity, then maybe they could figure out where the hell she and Rikki were. It would take Chase a good 45 minutes to get the necklace and get to Angel's, so Phoenix decided now was a good time to go beat the shit out of something.

Nodding once at Angel, he turned and walked out of the room. Going up the stairs and into one of the guest bedrooms, he quickly changed into some shorts he found in one of his bags. He was going to hurt someone if he didn't get rid of some of his anger. As Phoenix slammed out the back door, he heard Nico call his name. He just kept walking toward the barn. He could not talk. Could not breathe. Phoenix walked into the barn, grabbed the tape off a shelf, and started wrapping up his knuckles. Nico came in behind him. Not saying a word, they walked over to the punching bag. Nico held it while Phoenix pounded the piss out of it. After thirty minutes, he finally stopped, grabbed a towel, and wiped the sweat off his face and the blood off his hands. Then, while Nico waited by the door, Phoenix dropped to his knees in the middle of the old barn and prayed. He prayed for the life of his mate, the life of his sister, and his own soul if anything were to happen to either of them.

Once they got back to the house, Nico went to check in with Angel while Phoenix took a quick shower. After Phoenix was done, he headed back down the basement stairs towards the conference room. He heard a loud roar when he hit the bottom landing. Sounded to Phoenix like Jeremiah Black had shown up and he was one pissed off bear. Phoenix entered the conference room, took a seat at the table with the rest of his team, and waited for the bear to find his way to them. It did not take long.

"Where is my mate," Jeremiah growled as he stood at the entrance of the room. Wow, he was one big grizzly. As Phoenix watched, Jeremiah's fangs dropped and his eyes turned bear. He had never seen a bear shifter before. Only wolf and cat.

"Knock it off, Jeremiah," Angel growled. "You can't shift in here, dammit. You are too freaking big. Get yourself under control and sit your ass down."

Jeremiah continued to growl, but he visibly pulled his bear back and took a seat by one of RARE's team members, Trace. While they waited for Chase to arrive with the necklace, Angel gave Jeremiah a rundown on everything that had happened.

Once she was done, Jeremiah asked in a low deadly voice, "You mean to tell me that some sick fuck has Rikki and wants to breed her? My mate?"

"The General wants to breed Serenity. If he is aware of Rikki's gifts, then I am sure he will want to use her, too. We are not going to let that happen, though." Angel told him.

"You said they have had her for four days, Angel," he growled. "Four days! How can you tell me that something hasn't happened to her already?"

Just then there was a noise up in the kitchen. A moment later, Chase stood in the doorway. His Beta, Bran, was right behind him. Chase held up the necklace for everyone to see. "I got it. Let's hope this works."

As he moved over towards Angel, Phoenix got a glimpse of the necklace. He swallowed hard and then ground out, "A Phoenix. It's a Phoenix."

Chase nodded. "She told Summer a shaman made it for her a few years ago. He told her the phoenix was her future and would keep her safe."

"Find her, Angel," Phoenix ordered through clenched teeth. "You find Serenity, now. I'm ready to start hunting."

Angel nodded. Looking over at Chase she held her hand out for the necklace.

Chapter 6

Serenity cautiously peered around the dimly lit room keeping her eyes closed most of the way. She was not sure where she was and wanted a chance to assess the situation before letting whomever else was in the room know she was awake.

"You're back with the land of the living," a voice whispered as a hand gently moved her long dark hair out of her face. Serenity's brown eyes flew open and she stared up into the face of the woman that she had saved. "Your fever is gone."

"Are they watching us?" Serenity whispered. She sat up and gingerly scooted back to lean against the wall. Titling her head back, she took in a deep breath, before letting it out again. The pain in her chest was now just a dull ache.

"I checked the room out. I did not find any cameras or bugs, but that doesn't mean they aren't here," the woman responded. "Some scientists were here earlier. They checked your temperature, took some of your blood, and left. That was it."

Serenity nodded. Her head was pounding. But, after what she had just been through, she could deal with it. She just wished she had the ability to heal herself, too. Unfortunately, no matter how often she had tried in the past, it just was not possible. She could heal others all day long, but when it came to herself, she could not even heal a paper cut. "I understand. At least all they did was take my blood this time. It could have been worse. Who are you?"

"Rikki, my name is Rikki. I was on the team that came to rescue the women from the facility you were being held in. Unfortunately, we both ended up here...wherever here is," Rikki said as she gazed around the room. "How are you feeling? You were pretty out of it. You had me worried for a bit."

"Groggy, tired, but the pain in my chest is almost gone," Serenity whispered. "I have a headache, but I'll be fine soon. I would be perfect if I could just shift, but I refuse to give the General the satisfaction of seeing me go furry."

Rikki let out a deep breath and closed her eyes. "Thank God. I don't understand why you did it, but I am pretty sure you saved my life. If you hadn't done whatever you did, I would probably be dead by now. No one lifted a finger to help me until you. With all the scientists around here, you would think someone could have stitched me up. "

"It's ok," Serenity lied. No it really was not ok. Serenity was so screwed and she knew it. At least before she had let her healing ability be known, she'd had more of a chance of going unnoticed. Now the General would want the scientists to not only keep a close eye on her, but she would also be subjected to horrible experiments. Maybe she would get lucky and it would keep her out of the mommy pool longer. She was sure the General would want to breed her because of her abilities, but he would want to run tests on her first to see exactly what she was capable of doing. It would give Phoenix more time to find her, if he was even looking.

"No, it is not ok," Rikki said angrily. "The General knows about your healing ability now. He obviously didn't before, but now he does. I am sure that's why they came in and took your blood earlier."

Serenity squeezed her eyes shut tightly as she cursed under her breath. "He would have found out sooner or later," she said after a moment. "It is what it is."

Rikki watched her closely as she said, "You told me that you did it for Phoenix. Do you know Phoenix?"

Serenity looked up at her warily. She did not know this woman. She wasn't sure if she should say anything to her or not. Deciding to trust her instincts she told her, "He's my mate. I have never met him, but Ashley told me he was coming for me and that he is mine."

"Oh shit," Rikki hissed. "You're sure?" Serenity swallowed hard and then nodded. Rikki sat quietly for a minute and then she started laughing. "Let me tell ya something, girl. As soon as Phoenix finds out about you, he will hunt you down, he will find you, and he will blow the fuck apart anybody and anything that gets in his way. The General made a huge mistake when he decided to take you."

"But Phoenix doesn't even know about me," Serenity told her in surprise. "Oh, I guarantee you, if he doesn't know about you yet, he will soon," Rikki responded with a grin. " And I promise you, Serenity, that I will do anything and everything that I can to keep you safe until my brother gets to you."

"Your brother?" Serenity asked in surprise. Rikki laughed, "He might as well be my brother. He and Nico saved me when nobody else gave a damn. They were there for me when I needed them. My team is my family and Phoenix and Nico are my brothers. I would do anything for them. And I will do anything for you, Serenity, because you just became a part of our family and we protect what is ours."

Serenity swallowed hard and then whispered, "Thanks. It's been a long time since anyone has cared about me."

Just then Serenity felt a pushing sensation in her mind and froze. Oh hell no. This was not happening. "What's wrong," Rikki asked, glancing around quickly.

"Someone is trying to get into my head. I can't let that happen. I won't. The General can go fuck himself if he thinks he is going to get to me that way," Serenity growled. She curled up into a little ball with her forehead on her knees, arms wrapped around her legs, and started rocking back and forth fighting to keep the presence out. She absolutely refused to let anyone into her mind. No one was going to take control of her. Not ever again.

"Wait! It might be Angel," Rikki said as she scrambled over beside her. Reaching out, she grabbed Serenity's shoulders shaking her. Thank God most of the pain was gone already, or that would have hurt.

"Angel?" Serenity questioned. She could feel the determination by the other person to break down her wall. Damn, whoever it was, they were good. And Serenity would know. She had spent months trying to keep a very talented sadistic bastard from mind raping her. This person had a lot of power. She did not think she could hold out much longer.

"Yes, Angel. She is the alpha of my team. She can slip in and out of people's minds. I have been waiting for her to try and connect with me, but she hasn't. Maybe she is connecting with you? Although, I'm not sure how since she has never met you before. Maybe it's through Phoenix somehow?"

Serenity growled as pain sliced through her head. "I'm not letting anyone in my head, Rikki. If it's her, she can get the hell out and find you."

"You want to just sit here and wait for the General to come back? You want to lay back and spread your legs for whatever scumbag he sends your way?" Rikki yelled. "Put on some fucking big girl panties, Serenity, and see who it is. If it isn't Angel, then just kick them back out and slam a wall in place. Do it, dammit."

Serenity gritted her teeth and glared at Rikki. If she didn't know that Rikki was right and that this might be their ticket to freedom, she would have decked her. She may have been all sweet and innocent in the past, but that had all changed once Malcolm had started stalking her. She still had her weak moments, just like everyone else, but now was not one of them. Rikki was right. Serenity took a deep breath, closed her eyes, and yanked up her big girl panties.

The pain in her head suddenly receded as Serenity allowed the presence into her mind. The feeling was a soft and gentle sensation, not the fast and brutally painful way that Malcolm had always used.

Who are you? Serenity growled at the intruder. Show no fear. She had learned that from Malcolm, too. Showing her fangs, Serenity continued to growl.

Back down, pup, a female voice demanded. *I am here to help.* When Serenity didn't respond, the female let out a frustrated growl herself. *Look, I don't want to hurt you because that would just piss Phoenix off, but if you don't stand down, trust me, I will make you.*

Serenity froze. She did not say a word, she just sat there waiting; but she did stop growling. This woman knew Phoenix. That meant she was probably Angel. Yet life had taught Serenity not to take anything for granted. Unfortunately, she had learned many life lessons over the past five years since the death of her parents. Things had been difficult without her father there to guide and protect her, but Serenity was a survivor. Hell, she had survived Malcolm. She could get through this, too.

Smart little wolf, aren't you? the voice said. *Is Rikki with you?* Serenity still did not respond. *You don't trust me, do you? I don't blame you. I'm not sure how much longer I can hold our connection, so let me talk fast. I am Angel, leader of RARE. Rikki is a part of my team. We busted up the General's little party at his largest facility, but in the process, Rikki got shot saving Nico's ass. Then the General stole both of you. Now, I need to know where you are because some Ashley chic told Phoenix that you are his mate and he is about to tear apart everyone and everything to get to you. Got it?*

Serenity took a deep breath, savoring the knowledge that not only did Phoenix know about her, but he was trying to find her. He was coming for her. There was just one problem. She had no idea where she was. She had just woken up not too long ago. She wasn't even sure how long she had been out.

Letting a small amount of her own power out, she helped Angel hold the connection between them. *I'm not going to be much help. I just woke up. I have no clue where we are.*

It's been four days, Serenity. They kept you drugged that long? Angel asked in confusion. *Why would they keep you drugged the whole time? Is that why I can't reach, Rikki? Is she drugged, too?*

No, I wasn't drugged. I was just...out of it, Serenity told her. She never told anyone about her healing abilities. One more life lesson she had learned.

When she was a child, Serenity had used her ability to help heal her friend who had fallen out of a tree and ended up with a broken arm. The little girl had been in so much pain. Serenity had not known what she was doing. All she knew was that her friend was hurt and crying and she wanted to take the pain from her. Serenity had reached out and grasped her arm by the break. The girl had screamed, but Serenity did not let go. She had felt the power rise up in her and it seemed to jump from her hand to the other girl's arm.

Then it was as if she had absorbed all of the other girl's pain. She took it all in until the girl stopped crying. Serenity had not healed the break fully that time, but she did catch the attention of the pack's healer.

From that moment on, anytime anyone was hurt beyond the normal every day cut or bruise, they called on Serenity to heal them. No one seemed to care how much pain or trauma it caused her. When her parents realized Serenity would not be able to handle much more, they had taken her and ran.

Serenity pulled her thoughts away from the past. There would be time later to dwell on things that she could not change, right now she needed to worry about the things she could. *Let me talk to Rikki and see if she remembers anything. She was in so much pain when we got here, though, that it is doubtful.*

Serenity hesitated for a moment. *I want to see him*, she finally said. *Please, I want to see my mate. Just for a second, then I will let you go.*

Angel hesitated before responding, *Of course.* Serenity took a deep breath and then instead of Angel being in her mind, she was in Angel's and seeing out of her eyes. As she watched, Angel looked over at the most beautiful man Serenity had ever seen. He was leaning up against a wall with his arms crossed over his chest and his dark, skull trimmed head bowed. He had on a tight black tee shirt that showed off his muscular arms and stomach and she could see a tattoo peeking out from under his shirt collar. Serenity thought tattoos were sexy as sin. She hoped Phoenix did, too, because she had one of her own.

As she watched, Phoenix lifted his head and looked at Angel. His gorgeous blue eyes were filled with so much pain. Serenity wanted to make the pain go away. Her mate should not be hurting like this.

Angel didn't move, she just continued to stand there letting Serenity watch Phoenix. Phoenix's eyes narrowed. "Angel, you ok? Did you talk to Serenity? Do you know where the General is holding them?"

"Serenity is right here with me, Phoenix," Angel said, still not moving. "She wanted to see you." Phoenix froze, his eyes widening. Then he slowly walked towards Angel. When he stood right in front of her, Serenity could not resist. She took over Angel's mind, and raising Angel's arm she ran her hand over the top of Phoenix's head and down the side of his cheek. Then she slowly traced a tattoo that ran down his arm.

Distantly she heard growling, but she could not seem to stop herself. *Mine*, she whispered. She wanted to sink her fangs in his neck and claim him right there. She wanted the world to know that he was hers. As she opened her mouth, Angel yanked back control. *That is enough, pup. You really don't want me to claim your mate, do you?* Well, when you put it that way, hell no.

As Angel backed away from Phoenix, Serenity became more aware of the commotion in the room. Two men were holding another man back whom seemed to be trying to get to Angel and Phoenix, and he was pissed. His eyes were pure wolf and he looked close to shifting. *It's ok,* Angel told her. *Chase gets a little possessive sometimes. But then, no one likes to watch their mate feel up another man and then try to claim him.*

Serenity took one last look at Phoenix as he stood there in confusion. *I will make contact after I talk to Rikki,* was all she said as she slid back out of Angel's mind.

Chapter 7

After Serenity broke the connection, Angel walked over to where Chase was struggling to get control of himself. "Stop it, ass hat," she told him. "That was Serenity, not me. Do you really think I would touch Phoenix like that?" Angel reached out and put her hand on Chase's chest to try to calm him. She gently stroked his arm with her other hand when she felt him lean into her touch. Chase slowly got control of his wolf and then he turned and walked as far away from Angel as he could get and still be in the room. Uh oh, Angel thought. This could be bad.

Chase was Angel's mate. Angel had known since the day they met, but she did not want a mate. She had too many issues in her past, too many ghosts, and too many enemies to accept a mate into her life. As much as she wanted to be the woman Chase wanted, she knew she could not. She needed to deny him to keep him safe.

Shaking her head, she turned and went to sit down at the table. "Well, I found out a few things. First of all, Rikki is fine. Serenity was fighting me the whole time, but I got impressions of her somehow healing Rikki. She has an ability that the General is going to be very interested in studying. Second thing, Serenity is strong as hell. She might be tiny, but she is a firecracker. After she finally let me in, she held the link most of the time. It didn't even seem to drain her. When she asked to see Phoenix, and I let her into my mind, she took over. That was Serenity touching you, Phoenix. She almost had me claim you before I was able to get control back from her. I hate to admit this, but she could be stronger than I am. I don't think I would have gotten into her mind if she hadn't decided to let me in."

"Do you have any idea where they are?" Jeremiah asked. It was obvious he was still having trouble controlling his bear. His mate was missing and he wanted answers yesterday.

"No," Angel said wearily. "Serenity didn't know. Seems she just woke up. If she has been out for the whole four days, then her healing ability must take a lot out of her. She is going to talk to Rikki to see if she remembers anything and then get back with me."

"She can just merge back with you at any time?" Nico wanted to know. "Without even knowing you or having anything of yours with her?"

"What can I say?" Angel shrugged. "The girl's got skills."

"Did you learn anything else from her?" Jaxson asked, hoping for some ideas as to where to look next.

"Only that Phoenix is beautiful and she loves his sexy tats," Angel responded.

Chase got up and headed towards the door. "I need to get back to work. Bran can stay and help you as long as you need him." Without waiting for a response, Chase was out the door and up the stairs. Angel quickly followed and caught up with him outside by his car. She needed to talk to him. Angel knew he was pissed, and she could not leave things the way they were.

"Chase, stop this," Angel demanded. " It wasn't me and you know it."

"This time it wasn't," Chase growled. "You don't want this, Angel. You don't want a mate, and you don't want me. And I can't seem to stay the fuck away from you."

"I just can't right now, Chase." Angel whispered. "I need to concentrate on getting Rikki and Serenity home."

"And then what, Angel? What excuse will you come up with next? You haven't even been by to see Faith and Hope since you got home. They miss you. Hell, I miss you." RARE had recently raided one of the General's facilities where two women and three children were being held. Angel had quickly become attached to two of the children, Faith and Hope. Chase had agreed to let them live with him knowing that Angel was not able to take care of the girls while she was away on missions. However, Angel was to come see them and help care for them when she was home. She hadn't been by since her last mission had gone to shit. Not only that, but she hadn't spoken with or seen Chase either.

Angel didn't know what to say. Chase was her mate. She hadn't been looking for one. She didn't want one. But it was hard for mates to be apart. It had been four days since her last mission. That was a long time not to be near each other. The distance was even more difficult to endure as neither Chase nor Angel had been claimed by one another.

"I'm sorry, Angel. I can't do this anymore," Chase growled. Reaching out he gently stroked a finger down her face before stepping back. "You get your life in order and if you decide that you can handle me in it, let me know. I might still be around. Until then, this is goodbye."

Angel's wolf went crazy. No way in hell was she letting Chase go. Angel growled and she felt her fangs drop. He was hers. What the hell did he mean he might still be around? She moved towards him as he opened his car door. "What do you mean you might be around? Is there someone else, Chase?" she growled.

"What if there was?" he asked. "Would you even care? I doubt it." As he moved to get in the car, Angel grabbed him and swung him around. Shoving him up against the car, she moved her body in close, caging him in.

"Is there someone else?" she demanded again. There better not be. She would tear her apart limb by limb. He was hers, dammit!

Chase growled low in his throat. He was the Alpha. No one touched him like this. Angel was not backing down, though. Not that her wolf would let her. "There will be no one else, Chase. No one. Ever."

Chase pushed her away as he turned to get in the car, and Angel could not hold back any longer. Moving quickly she grabbed his arm and swung him around. She pulled his head back, pushed him back harder against the car, and yanking his shirt collar down, she sunk her teeth into his shoulder. Right now all she could think about was staking her claim. She would worry about the consequences later.

"What the fuck," Chase roared as he grabbed a handful of her hair trying to yank her head back. Angel was not letting go of him or his shoulder. After a moment he just stood there. When Angel pulled back licking at the claiming mark, she suddenly realized how still Chase was. She froze. Oh my God, what had she done? She had just claimed her mate, the Alpha of a wolf pack, up against his car in her driveway *and without his permission*. But he was her mate; he would want her, right?

She nervously stepped back and looked up at him. He stared at a space over her shoulder. "Chase," she whispered as she reached out a hand towards him.

"Do not touch me," he growled, his whole body shaking. Turning, Chase, got in his car and drove away. Well wasn't that just craptastic? Swearing under her breath, Angel headed back toward the house.

Chapter 8

Serenity sat silently for several minutes with her eyes closed memorizing every detail she could remember of Phoenix. She could still feel the soft stubble of his hair on the palm of her hand. Could still smell his musky, earthy scent that had driven her wolf wild. And his tattoos...Serenity shuddered and let out a small moan. She wanted to lick every one of them, starting with the one on his chest and moving down.

"Are you ok?" she heard Rikki ask. Slowly Serenity shoved her dark hair back out of her face and looked up at Rikki, who was kneeling on the floor in front of her, an expression of concern on her face.

Serenity nodded. Swallowing hard, trying not to cry at the feeling of hopelessness that ran through her, she answered. "Yeah. Just took a trip through Angel's mind and saw Phoenix. Trying to come back to reality."

Rikki threw a fist pump in the air. "Yes! I know it was Angel. When are they coming for us? I am ready to get the hell out of here."

Serenity started shaking her head. "They aren't, Rikki. They have no idea where we are. Do you remember anything that might help them find us? I was so drugged, all I remember is being put in the helicopter, flying, and then waking up and seeing you in so much pain. Heck, Angel said I was out for four days. I don't remember anything."

Rikki thought for a minute and then slowly shook her head. "Not right now. Give me some time to think about it. I remember being shot, and then I must have passed out. I woke up a couple of times in the chopper and again when we landed, but I was pretty out of it. I remember it was hot. I was sweating. But that could have been from a fever."

Serenity looked over at the cot and back at Rikki. She wanted to rest, but didn't know how to ask Rikki to watch over her. It had been years since she had trusted anyone to do anything for her. Asking someone to protect her while she slept was scary as hell. But then, hadn't Rikki already been doing that for the last four days?

Before she could say anything, Rikki gestured towards the cot. Lowering her voice Rikki said, "Rest, girl. I know you still aren't 100 percent and connecting with Angel had to have taken a lot out of you. We need you to get better if we are going to escape from here, wherever here is. We can't afford to sit around and wait for RARE to save us. Get some sleep."

Smiling weakly at Rikki, Serenity moved to the cot and climbed up onto it. Rikki settled down beside the cot so that she was within reach if Serenity needed her. "What's up with the gloves?" Serenity asked as she reached out and lightly touched one of Rikki's gloved hands. Rikki shook her head once and looked away. Understanding dawned on Serenity as her eyes widened. They still did not know if they were being watched. Neither of them had thought about that as Serenity had connected to Angel.

Thinking back, she decided that even if the scientists had been watching, unless they could hear what was being said, they would not have known what was going on. The whole time she had been speaking with Angel, Serenity's head had been down on her knees giving nothing away.

Praying that there weren't any listening devices in the room, Serenity finally let herself drift off to sleep dreaming of Phoenix's beautiful bright blue eyes.

****

As Rikki guarded Serenity, she tried to remember any little detail that would help her team find them. There had to be something that she could tell them, she just had to remember. She thought back to the day they were taken and remembered shoving Nico down the ridge. Then there was a sharp pain in her chest. The bullet had hit her closer to her shoulder then her chest, but the fiery pain had engulfed both areas. She had passed out and when she had regained consciousness she was in the chopper. The pain had been excruciating. She remembered trying to breathe through it while looking around to get an idea of where she was. She saw the pilot up front with the General. Serenity was in the back with Rikki and two guards. Then she had passed out again. She came to one more time on the chopper and then again when they had landed in the desert. Holy shit, she and Serenity were in a desert.

Chapter 9

Phoenix sat on Angel's back porch quickly sketching a picture in his notebook. She had beautiful long dark hair flowing down her back, with tiny porcelain-like facial features, eyes closed. Her eyes were always closed when he sketched her. He had never seen them open. Her head was tilted back and her mouth slightly open. She had been so still.

He felt someone enter the room as he started shading in Serenity's hair. It was just one of several notebooks he had filled with sketches of her over the past few days. He had even sketched several pictures of wolves, trying to capture what she might look like in wolf form. He was going with dark brown or black because of her dark hair. Serenity had become his obsession.

Nico walked in from the kitchen and placed a hand on Phoenix's shoulder. "We are going to get her back, my brother. Angel talked to her, man. She's damn strong. If she could take over Angel even for a minute, she is one strong woman. A woman you can be proud of. She is going to fight to get to you, Phoenix."

Phoenix raised his head and glared at Nico. "Don't you think I know that, Nico? She is strong. She is smart. She is also at the mercy of that monster, the General. It doesn't matter how strong she is. If he wants to hurt her, he will."

Nico tightened his grip on Phoenix's shoulder. "You just remember what happened in that basement a little bit ago, Phoenix. Your mate not only took over Angel's mind to connect with you physically, she almost had Angel mark you. That is one determined wolf. She wants you, and nothing is going to stand in her way. If she can take over Angel like that, who knows what else she can do?"

Phoenix froze as he thought back. Serenity had actually made Angel touch him. She had forced her will on Angel. If she could do that to Angel, then maybe she could influence the people holding her. Just then, the porch door slammed against the wall as Angel walked in.

"Are you two going to sit there holding fucking hands all day, or are we going to do something to get Rikki and Serenity back?" Nico's eyebrows shot up as he inhaled deeply.

"Not a word. Not a fucking word," Angel ground out as she stormed past. "In the basement now."

As Nico rose to follow Angel back downstairs, Phoenix reached out a hand and lightly traced the facial features he had drawn of Serenity. "I am coming for you, Beauty. I'm coming."

When they were all once again in the conference room, Angel picked up the necklace and looked at it. It was made of brown leather and had an intricate design of a phoenix in black with flames behind it. It was just plain kick ass. As Phoenix watched, Angel sat down, held the necklace tightly in her hands and closed her eyes. About five minutes later she came back to them mad as hell.

"I can't get through," she growled as she stood up and started pacing. "I don't know why, but she isn't responding." All of the sudden she swung around and kicked her chair. It flew up off the floor and hit the wall leaving a hole where the wheel on the chair leg hit it.

"Calm down, Angel," Jaxson said. Angel grabbed him and swung him around, slamming him against the wall and baring her teeth at him. Jaxson barely controlled his wolf's response. His wolf was ready to fight, but this was Angel, his alpha. He did not know what he had done to piss her off, but as his alpha, she deserved his respect.

Jaxson tilted his head to the side, bared his neck in submission and waited. There was complete silence in the room. Nobody moved. Finally, Angel seemed to get control of her wolf. She let go of Jaxson and turned to walk out of the room. As she passed Phoenix, she handed him the necklace. No one followed her. They knew better. They all wanted to keep their balls intact, thank you very much.

Phoenix clenched the necklace in his hand, shutting his eyes tightly. He wished he could connect with Serenity. He wanted to hear her voice and to know that she was ok. He wanted to feel her hand on him again, without Angel in the way this time. Slowly he unclenched his hand and then slipped the necklace on. He would keep it safe for her until she could wear it again. Soon, he promised himself. Soon.

Chapter 10

Serenity woke up to the sound of angry voices in the room. "You are not getting near her again," she heard Rikki say. "You have stolen enough of her blood. You don't need anymore. Now get out."

"Look," she heard a placating voice whisper urgently. "I just need a little bit more. The General wants…."

"Does it look like I care what the General wants? No, you will get the fuck out of this room, now," Rikki told the scientist.

Holy shit, was Rikki really going up against the General? For her? But she was human, they would hurt her. Serenity could not let that happen. Keeping her eyes closed and her breathing even so it looked like she was still asleep, Serenity silently slipped into the scientist's mind with the intentions of making her leave empty-handed. She hated entering someone's personal space without permission after what Malcolm had done to her, but she would do whatever it took to keep Rikki safe.

Instantly, Serenity felt the raw terror in the young scientist's mind. The woman was so scared of the darkness that was to come if she could not get the blood from Serenity. The General threatened to put her back in the hole if she did not follow through with his orders. The scientist had spent most of her life in the hole and did not want to go back. Besides, if she did not get the blood, he would just send someone else to do it. Someone that would hurt one of the women, and she really did not want that. But the woman refused to ask for one of the guards to help. She would take her punishment before personally bringing pain to anyone.

She had such a kind and gentle soul. The soul of an omega. Omega wolves did not have a violent or dominant nature. They were able to feel the other people's emotions and their presence alone calmed them. There was no way in hell Serenity was letting the General send this woman back into the darkness.

Serenity pulled quietly back out of the young scientist's mind, and then opened her eyes and sat up. Rikki immediately moved over next to Serenity offering silent support and protection. Serenity motioned the scientist forward and rested her arm out, elbow up so she could get to the vein. Surprise flashed across the woman's face, but then she moved slowly forward and knelt down beside Serenity. "I am so sorry," she whispered as she got the needle ready.

"I know you are," Serenity told her. "Can anyone see or hear us?"

The woman kept her head down, her long hair covering her face, and said, "There is a video feed coming through, but no sound. This is an older building that the General hasn't used for years. I was surprised that you were brought here. Except for me, he moved all of the other women about five years ago. I have always been here." Fear evident in her voice the woman whispered, "He says he is saving me."

Serenity would think about that later. Right now she needed quick answers. "Where exactly are we?"

"I don't know for sure," the girl responded, her lips barely moving. "There are two guards here with me at all times, but sometimes one of them sneaks out to go to Las Vegas."

Filing that information away as the woman started gathering up the vials of blood, Serenity asked, "What's your name?"

"He calls me Six," was the response. "I didn't ask you what the General calls you. I asked you what your name is," Serenity told her softly.

The woman stood up and turned towards the door. Then she looked back at Serenity with tears in her dark green eyes. "Jade," she said softly. My name is Jade." Then she turned and rushed out of the room, shutting the door behind her.

Rikki sat down beside her on the cot, stretching out her legs. "Wanna tell me what that was all about?" she asked.

"Her name is Jade. She is not here because she wants to be. And she is not a scientist. Not a real one anyway. She's just doing what she was told to do. If not, the General has her beaten and stuck in a hole."

"A what?" Rikki exclaimed. "He puts her in a hole?"

"Yeah," Serenity sighed. "And she was ready to go back down in that hole for us if she had to. Did you remember anything while I was out? Jade says we are near Las Vegas."

Rikki looked over towards the door, then back at Serenity. "We are in a desert. I remembered that. We got out of the chopper in a desert."

"The Mojave Desert," Serenity realized. She had been through Las Vegas once years ago when she and her parents had been on the run from Malcolm. Las Vegas is in the Mojave Desert. Wrapping her arms around her legs, she rested her forehead on her knees. She did not want the guards to see the vacant look in her eyes that she would get while contacting Angel. She had some things to tell her.

Closing her eyes, Serenity attempted to slip into Angel's mind. It took her a few minutes to make contact. But when she did, she immediately felt pain and despair. Something was wrong. Angel was punching a bag and her knuckles were raw. There was blood flowing over her hands and down her arms.

Stop it! Serenity demanded. *Stop this right now. I don't know what is wrong, but you are only hurting yourself and we need you.*

Angel stopped beating the shit out of the bag and grabbed hold of it instead. She was shaking and the emotional pain she was in was suffocating her. Serenity gently stroked a soothing hand down her long blond hair trying to calm her. After a moment, Angel straightened and walked over to sit on a bale of hay. Hay? Serenity thought. Where the heck was Angel?

Talk to me, Serenity, Angel said after she got a hold of herself. *We are ready to come get you and Rikki. Where are we headed?*

Las Vegas, Nevada, Serenity informed her. *I'm not sure what you're up against, but I do know you are going to Las Vegas. We are in an older facility somewhere in the Mojave Desert. The guards sometime sneak out to Vegas, so we can't be far from there. They would want to be able to get back quickly if the General were to decide to show up.*

Ok, Angel responded. *Let me get the team gathered and we will roll out within 30 minutes. We are coming for you, Serenity. You tell Rikki, we are coming.*

Chapter 11

Severing their connection, Angel got up and quickly headed toward the house. She had a purpose now. She could worry about her jacked up life later. Hitting the stairs to the basement, Angel yelled, "Gear up! We are out of here in 10 minutes!"

Phoenix was the first one out the door. "Serenity?"

"She made contact. They are in the Mojave Desert by Vegas. Nico, call and get the plane ready. Jaxson, we need your techy ear comm devices because Jeremiah is going in with us. Jeremiah, if you have any contacts in that area, we need them. We are looking for an older building near enough to Vegas for the guards to sneak out for some action. Let's go people! Move!"

As everyone got busy packing things they would need to take, making phone calls, and gearing up, Angel turned towards Bran. "Tell Chase that we got a lead and are following through on it. Tell him thanks for the help."

"Wait," Bran said as Angel started to leave. When she turned back he continued, "I want to come with."

"You have a mate to take care of, Bran. Flame needs you here."

"No she doesn't. Flame doesn't want anything to do with me, Angel. She won't let me near her. The only thing that matters to her is revenge on the General. This is the only thing I can do for her right now. Help you track down that bastard and destroy him."

"What about your alpha?" Angel asked.

"I told Chase I wanted to join your team for now. He said he would pull Slade in to help while I'm gone. I am on loan to you indefinitely."

Well, shit, Angel thought. Screw her old rules. In the past Angel had refused to allow anyone to go on a mission with her team, but right now she would take help wherever she could get it. Besides, Bran might not be telepathic, but he was a bona fide badass. She would take him. "Well, what are you waiting for? Go gear up. We leave in 10." With that, she headed upstairs to her room to grab her own gear and get ready to go.

Ten minutes later the team was piled in an SUV and headed towards the hangar where they kept their plane. "I want an update. Where are we at?" Angel demanded.

"Plane will be ready when we get there, boss," Nico immediately responded.

"My contact in Vegas is sending a plane out to scout around. It's a plane disguised as a tourist attraction, so we shouldn't tip anyone off," Jeremiah said.

"I have an SUV waiting for us once we land in Vegas. We are landing at one of the smaller airstrips outside of town," Jaxson told them.

They arrived at the hangar five minutes later and exiting the SUV, they loaded into the jet. Jaxson and Phoenix went to the cockpit to pilot the plane while everyone else strapped in. Trace pulled out his sniper case and took out his gun to clean it. He had just cleaned it the day before, but it kept his hands busy and his mind off of other things. Right now all Trace wanted to think about was saving Rikki and Serenity. The rest of his fucked up life could wait.

Jeremiah sat across from him, his hands clenched tightly on the arm rests, a constant growl low in his throat. His hands clenched and unclenched on the arm rests, and his foot tapped in irritation. Jeremiah had no patience for an airplane ride. His mate was in trouble and he needed to be there for her. Leaning his head back against the seat, Jeremiah closed his eyes and brought up an image of his fearless, beautiful mate. Thoughts of holding Rikki soon was the only thing that helped keep him in control at the moment.

As the plane took off, Angel sat back in her seat and thought about Chase. She still could not believe she had marked him. He was hers, even though she did not want a mate. She hadn't been able to control her wolf when she had started thinking about him with someone else; but she should not have started the bonding process by taking him against his car. She had taken all of Chase's free will away. Either he was stuck with Angel, or he was alone. His wolf would not allow him to touch another female.

As Angel's wolf preened at that, Angel growled at her. She had no right to do what she had done. Now it would be even harder for them to be apart. And at this time, being together was not an option. Angel had to concentrate on getting Rikki and Serenity back, then she was taking down the General.

Chapter 12

"They're coming for us," Serenity told Rikki. "Angel said they are heading this way. We have to take Jade with us, Rikki. She doesn't belong here, and I refuse to let him stick her back in that hole! She is so afraid of him. He told her that he is saving her. For what, I don't know. But I am not going to let him have her!"

"She comes with us," Rikki agreed. Standing up, Rikki started prowling around the room. "I can't wait to get out of here. I am getting claustrophobic in this little room. Any idea how long it's going to take them?"

"No, and they still don't know exactly where we are. All I could tell them was that we are in the desert not far from Vegas. That's a lot of area to cover."

"You don't know my team. They will find us," Rikki promised.

"I got the impression that more than just your team is involved. I caught a thought from Angel that she was going to have a Jeremiah call in some favors from his contacts. Does that name mean anything to you?"

Rikki swung around and looked at her. "Jeremiah Black? He's helping Angel? That's strange. Jeremiah is FBI. I wouldn't think that Angel would contact him for help unless she absolutely had to."

"I got the impression that he is more than helping. He is part of the team looking for us. Something about he is one pissed off bear. It was just a fleeting thought that I caught." Serenity watched Rikki take in the news. There was such raw desire and hope on her face, Serenity knew her first impression had been right. Rikki was Jeremiah's mate, but she had no idea. Serenity kept her mouth shut, though, because it was not her place to tell Rikki. She would find out soon enough, but it would probably be best if Jeremiah told her.

As Rikki resumed her pacing, Serenity decided to check on Jade. Closing her eyes, she sought the mental path which would take her back to Jade's mind.

She was back in the hole surrounded by dark emptiness and she was terrified. Those bastards had put her back in there. Serenity immediately put her arms around her and stroked her hair humming softly. *It's ok, Jade. I am right here with you.*

Mommy? Jade asked. *Mommy, you found me?*

Serenity's heart clenched. How long had Jade been here? It was obvious she hadn't seen her mommy in years. Serenity kissed her softly on the head and whispered, *No, honey. It's Serenity. I am right here, though. Why are you back in the hole, Jade? What happened?*

A huge shudder ripped through Jade as she felt something slither over her foot. The guards had put snakes down with her this time. She knew they were harmless, they always were. But just the thought of snakes being there and Jade not being able to see them scared the hell out of her. What if a rattler got in and she couldn't tell the difference?

They saw me talking to you and wanted to know what I said. I told them that I had just talked you into giving me your blood, but they didn't believe me. They put me down here to try and break me. But it's not going to work. I hate them. I hate all of them. As another snake crawled up Jade's back and onto her shoulder, she started crying and shrunk in on herself.

Serenity wrapped her arms tighter around Jade and started to sing softly. The more she sang, the calmer Jade became. *My mom used to sing to me every night,* Jade whispered. *She would rock me and sing to me. Then one night they came and took me. I have been here ever since.*

How long have you been here, Jade? Serenity asked her.

Twenty years. I'm 24 now. I know because the General keeps a file on me and I sneak peeks at it sometimes. In the beginning there were scientists here that taught me to read and write. When the General was gone I would sit in the labs with them and learn whatever I could. When he was back, I was put down here. He said it was discipline. That I needed to learn to listen, Jade told her. *I tried to be good so that he wouldn't make me come back to the dark, but it never mattered how good I was.*

What about your wolf? Why don't you shift and let her help you? Serenity asked her.

I can't, Jade ground out as another huge shudder rippled through her. *The General doesn't know about her. He took me because he knows I'm telepathic. He wanted to train me and add me to his program when I was old enough. But the joke was on him because I am not a strong telepathic. I don't even know why he kept me. He says I will find out soon enough. Oh God, get them off me, Serenity, get them off!*

Serenity felt another snake crawling up Jade's leg. What was wrong with all of these sick bastards? Jade was an omega. She had the kindest, sweetest soul Serenity had ever seen. She would not hurt a fly if she could help it. *Do they have cameras down here?* She asked Jade.

No, but they glance down with a flash light a lot. Jade moaned loudly as a snake hissed right by her face.

Listen to me, Jade. I want you to let your wolf part way out. I can feel her fighting you. She wants to take care of you. Let her help you, Jade. You need to trust her. Omegas did not normally fight, but Jade's wolf had been pushed for so long that it was getting hard for Jade to keep her hidden. Jade slowly gave her wolf a little more control. All of the sudden her eyes opened going full wolf and her fangs dropped. She growled low in her throat and sensing a predator the snakes slithered into a corner away from Jade. *Good job, Jade. Now you sit here like this and those slimy things will stay far away from you.*

Jade swallowed hard. *Thanks, Serenity. I owe you...again.* She kept her eyes wolf watching the snakes, every once in a while letting out little growls.

Where is this hole, Jade? Serenity asked. She couldn't stand the thought of Jade being stuck in there much longer. They were not going to be able to wait for a rescue by RARE. They were going to have to make their own escape. They were getting Jade out of there now.

Outside behind the building. I am so scared. I know these snakes are harmless, but I hate it when the scorpions and rattlers show up. I have had to kill several.

A sense of foreboding filled Serenity. *Jade, when you killed them were you in your wolf form?*

Yeah, but not for long. Just long enough to get rid of them. No one's ever actually seen me change.

Oh hon, I have a feeling you are wrong. The General knows exactly what you are and that is why you are still alive. I have a feeling he has cameras hidden down in that hole somewhere. Don't you worry. Rikki and I are going to get out of here and we are taking you with us. We will come for you as soon as we can.

With that, Serenity swiftly broke the connection. Oh, yeah, she was sure the General knew about Jade. There was no other reason he would keep her, and if he was watching her that closely, then she was very important to him. Serenity was assuming that he wanted Jade for his breeding program and was just waiting for her to become stronger. He was probably hoping that her wolf would somehow help strengthen her telepathic gift. Serenity knew that Jade would never survive the breeding program. She was not strong enough. They had to get her out of there now.

Serenity quickly told Rikki about Jade and they agreed that they could not wait for RARE to escape. The only problem was getting out of their cell. The lock was on the outside of the door. Slowly Serenity started pacing around the room trying to come up with a plan. They tried several things. The first was banging on the door, yelling to get someone's attention with the idea of knocking them out once the door was opened. That did not work any better than the crying fit had. A couple of hours later they were still locked in the cell with no hope of escape.

All of the sudden Serenity grabbed her head and fell to the floor. Her body flopped as though in a seizure. Rikki cried out and ran over to her. Grabbing her arms, she tried to hold her down so that she could not hurt herself. Suddenly, the door opened and a guard rushed in. Within seconds, Serenity was on her feet slamming the guard against the wall, and wrestling his gun out of his holster.

As Rikki figured out what was happening, she grabbed the door before it could slam shut holding it open while Serenity knocked the guard out with the butt of his gun. Quickly, she searched the unconscious guard and found another gun and a knife. She and Rikki ran out of the room, making sure the door locked behind them. Serenity handed Rikki one of the guns and the knife. It would be hard enough for Serenity to kill anyone with a gun; there was no way she was doing it with a knife. Glancing up and down the dimly lit hall, they quickly realized they had no idea where to go. Crap, they should have thought this through more. Fear gripped both Serenity and Rikki as they realized they could end up right back in the cell they had just escaped from.

Serenity grabbed Rikki's arm and gestured for her to hold on a second. Closing her eyes, she sought out the telepathic path to Jade. *Jade, I need your help. We got out of the room, but now we don't know where to go.*

It took a minute, but then she received a response. *The General has six guards and two scientists at the facility. The labs are to the right but there isn't any way out that way, so go left. Remember left, right, left, right. That's what you want to do. Then you will be at the front door. Two guards will be there. One is out here, I can hear him. I have no idea where the other ones are.*

We're on our way, Jade! Serenity promised her. Serenity broke the connection and repeated the directions to Rikki. They took off running, slowing down when they got to the first right. Peering around the corner, they did not see any guards, so they took off again. When they took the next left they came face to face with two guards. Not even stopping, Serenity and Rikki both lifted their guns and fired. Three down, three to go.

Chapter 13

The team had ridden ATV's into the desert within 2 miles of the building where they were sure Rikki and Serenity were being held. Now they were slowly moving in, watching closely for signs of guards. They had been surprised on the last mission and lost one of their own to the enemy. Having Rikki shot and kidnapped by the General's men while being helpless to stop it was something the team would never forget. They were not going to let that happen again. Trace and Bran were in the back of the building, Phoenix and Angel in the front. Jeremiah and Jaxson were on the east side, and Nico was on the west.

"Anything?" Angel asked softly. They had been slowly making their way towards the building for the last ten minutes. All was quiet. "Nothing," was the unanimous response.

"Ok, let's…" before Angel could get anything else out the front door slammed open and two people ran out. As they watched, a guard ran out after them with his gun raised and one of them swung around and put a bullet in his head. "Well, maybe they didn't need our help after all," Angel said. But the women didn't stop. They ran as one around to the back of the building. "Trace, Rikki and Serenity are coming your way. I repeat, they are coming your way. Do not fire!"

"Got it," Trace responded. "Someone else is back here, boss. I can smell his rank ass from all the way over here. I'm going in for a closer look." Trace silently stalked the figure that looked like he was standing guard over a hole in the ground. What the hell? He heard Rikki and Serenity coming around the side of the building, but they stopped when they saw Trace.

Trace ignored them and kept creeping up on the guard who was facing the other way, smoking a cigarette and laughing at something in the ground. As Trace moved closer, he took a deep breath trying to figure out what was in that hole. One lung full was all it took, then Trace was shifted into his huge black cat and he attacked the guard. In seconds the guard was dead. Trace stood at the edge of the hole peering into wide dark green eyes. He lifted his head and roared, then he prowled around the circle trying to figure out how to get down to her. The hole was wider, but it was deep. Trace's cat had taken over and no matter how hard he tried, he could not yank that control back.

"Please, help me," the terrified woman whispered. "Get me out of here." The stark fear in her voice was too much. Not thinking twice, Trace jumped into the hole with her. Now the team would have to figure out how to get them both out, but at least she would not be alone. She scooted back against the wall of dirt and pointed to something behind him. That was when he heard the hiss and rattle. A rattlesnake threatened her. With another loud roar, he swung a powerful paw at the snake and sliced through its body with a thick claw. Nothing was going to hurt this green eyed beauty. Nothing.

Growling lowly, he paced around in a circle threatening anything that came too close. She huddled up against the wall watching him. Then she held out her arms. He could not resist. Trace moved to her and curled around her placing his head on her lap. She wrapped her arms around his neck burying her face in his fur. "Thank you," she whispered. "Thank you." Shuddering, Trace pressed closer. *Mine,* he thought, *mine.* Inhaling, Trace shuddered again and closed his eyes at the pure pleasure that raced through him.

"Trace," he heard a voice call down. He didn't bother to acknowledge the presence above. "Trace, answer me dammit. Are you alright?" He growled softly, and leaned back rubbing his nose on the woman's cheek. "I will take that as a yes."

"Jade," he heard another voice call. "Honey, are you ok?"

The woman next to him laughed softly as she stroked his fur. "I am now," she whispered. Tilting her head up she called, "Yeah, I'm good, thanks to Trace. I wasn't a few minutes ago. There was a rattler down here, but it didn't stand a chance once Trace jumped to my rescue."

There was a chuckle and then the other voice called down, "There is a rope ladder up here. We are going to send it down so you can climb out. And, Trace, Nico has some extra clothes we are going to throw down for you. They should work for now."

Trace could not help it. He started growling again. Even though he knew he was being unreasonable, he did not want Jade going up that ladder without him. If she went up without him, he would not be able to protect her. It didn't matter that his whole team was waiting at the top.

Jade glanced down at him and smiled. "How about I wait for you to change and then we go up together?" Trace purred, rubbing his head against her shoulder. "Ok," she said as she let out another laugh. "That's what we'll do."

His clothes hit the ground and then the ladder was lowered into the hole. Raising his head he, growled at the others who were looking over the edge. "Come on, Trace," Nico hollered. "Let Jade climb up here. Then you can follow."

"We will be up in a minute," Jade called back. "Can everyone move back so he can change, please?"

As Trace watched, everyone backed away from the edge of the hole. Everyone except Angel; she was watching Jade closely. He moved back from Jade and started to shift, but she grabbed him. "Don't you dare shift while another woman is watching," she hissed. He stopped and looked up at Angel waiting for her to leave.

"Shift and get up here, Trace. We need to beat feet back to the ATVs," Angel ordered as she moved away from the top of the hole.

Trace glanced over and waited until Jade nodded. As she watched the top of the hole making sure no one came back, he shifted and pulled on his borrowed pants. They were a little loose, but would work for now. Reaching out, Trace tugged Jade close, wrapping his arms around her and holding her tightly. Trace shivered as Jade leaned back and lightly skimmed a hand from the top of his shoulder, down his dark muscular chest to stop at the top of his jeans. Her pale white skin was so light next to the dark color of his. "I think I like tattoos," she whispered as she reached out again to trail a finger over the one going down his arm.

"We better get going," he finally said gruffly, reaching down and grabbing his shirt off the ground and pulling it on.

"I'll go up first and you come up right behind me," Trace told her. "I need to make sure it is safe for you before you come over the top."

Jade nodded and Trace started climbing. He stopped and waited until she was right behind him before continuing up the ladder. When he reached the top he saw half of the team waiting for them, along with Rikki and another woman he assumed was Serenity. He crawled over the edge and turned back around for Jade, pulling her up and placing himself between Jade and his team.

Finally, clear of that fucking hole in the ground, Trace was able to get his first good look at Jade. She was gorgeous. Beautiful long blond hair, dark green eyes, soft full lips. As he looked closer, his eyes widened in shock. Taking her chin in his hand he moved her face to the side and then back again. What the hell? He turned his stunned gaze from Jade to Angel. "Angel, you better come over here."

"Angel?" Jade mouthed silently turning towards the figure moving her way. Angel stopped in front of her and reached out a hand to lightly caress Jade's face. "Mom," Jade whispered. Trace watched as Angel's eyes filled with tears. Was she really Jade's mom? He had been a part of RARE for nearly five years now, and she had never insinuated that she might have a daughter out there.

Suddenly the sound of a helicopter filled the air; this little family reunion was going to have to wait. They need to roll out now! Grabbing Jade's hand he yelled, "Let's move!" Angel took one last look at Jade and then turned to head towards the ATVs. "I'm trusting you to help me protect my daughter, Trace," she told him through the comms. "Stay close to me so that I can keep an eye on her." Trace did not bother to respond. There was no doubt in his mind he would give his life for Jade, whether Angel was her mother or not.

Chapter 14

Phoenix had watched Serenity come flying out of the building, gun in hand, holding it like a pro. She had been with Rikki, and when the two of them had taken off towards the back of the building, Angel had immediately followed them, so he knew she was safe for now. The need to get to her was almost overwhelming, but he had a job to do. He knew his team would protect her until he could. Right now, he had a building to wire.

As Phoenix was setting the last explosive in place, he heard the thump, thump, thump of a chopper's propellers. Through his ear comm he heard Angel yell that they were moving out. "Let me know when everyone's clear," he ground out. It was killing him that he could not be with Serenity. He was the only one who could set the building to blow, but even knowing that, it was hard to make himself stay where he was and concentrate on what needed to be done. Phoenix wanted to be with Serenity, be there to protect her. To tell her that she was going to be safe and the General and his men were never going to get near her again. But that would have to wait.

Just as he finished, Phoenix looked up and saw the chopper coming in fast and low. Oh, fuck, this did not look good. "Get out of there, Phoenix," he heard Angel yell. "Get out of there now!" Phoenix took off at a dead run towards a building a good 50 yards away. He was still a few yards out when the helicopter let a missile fly. It slammed into the building Phoenix had just wired. With the added explosives Phoenix had set, it blew it sky high. The force of the explosion picked Phoenix up and hurled him through the air, slamming him against the other building. Shit that hurt.

Phoenix pushed himself onto his knees, pain screaming through his chest and ribs. He tried to stand, using the building for support, but he was too dizzy and the pain was crippling. He fell back down on his ass and scooted up against the side of the building, breathing deeply to try and stop his head from spinning.

Phoenix watched as the chopper landed and two men got out. Come a little closer you fuckers Phoenix thought as he pulled the gun from the holster on his thigh. Reaching up with his left hand, he wiped the blood out of his eyes. Squinting, he tried to keep the men in his sights as he gripped the Glock tightly. All he could think about was killing the bastards so they did not get to Serenity. There was no way he was letting them take her back.

As Phoenix waited for the men to get close enough so he could do some damage, a small black wolf flew out from behind the building tackling one of them. The wolf wasn't very big, but the man wasn't expecting it and he went down easily. Not pausing, the wolf sank its teeth into his throat and bit down hard tearing it out. Phoenix raised his gun trying to get a bead on the other guy moving towards the wolf. Just as the man reached the wolf, Phoenix pulled the trigger and dropped the bastard to the ground.

The wolf came over to Phoenix, lying at his feet whining softly. Looking into the captivating brown eyes, Phoenix reached out and gently stroked her head. "Serenity?' he questioned softly somehow knowing it was her. Pushing her head into his palm, Serenity let a sound of pleasure rumble in her throat. "Thank you, my Beauty," he whispered to his mate. "Let's get out of here." Groaning softly, Phoenix once again pushed himself up into a standing position. Just as he began to slide back down, he felt someone grab him and pull him back up.

"I gotcha, buddy," Nico said. Phoenix cursed as Nico pulled his arm up around Nico's shoulders and slipped his own arm around Phoenix's back. "Talk to me. What's the damage?"

"Busted ribs, concussion, and something's stuck in my leg," Phoenix muttered. "Let's go. Gotta get Serenity out of here." As they started moving towards where they had left the ATV's, Serenity yipped. When they turned around, she took off towards the running helicopter. Turning back around, she yipped again. Why not? Phoenix thought.

As Phoenix and Nico followed Serenity to the helicopter, Jaxson and Bran came out from behind the building and ran their way. Once they reached the helicopter, Jaxson and Bran jumped up front to pilot, while Nico and Phoenix sat down in back. Serenity jumped into the chopper and crawled over to Phoenix resting her head on his leg. He gently stroked her head and neck as Nico checked out his thigh where a piece of tin was sticking out of it from the roof of the building that Phoenix had blown. Phoenix sunk his fingers into Serenity's soft fur and tightened his grip as the chopper lifted off the ground.

"This might have hit an artery," Nico told him. "I'm going to wait to take it out until we get to our plane just in case. I'll tape your ribs up then too." Phoenix nodded and leaned back closing is eyes. He was so tired. He had not slept in days, and now that Serenity was near, he could not stay awake. "Oh, no you don't, brother," Nico said shaking Phoenix back awake. "You don't get to pass out with a concussion."

Serenity whined, licking his hand and nipping at it. He chuckled softly, "It's all good, Beauty. I promise not to pass out on you. Why don't you change back and talk to me?"

"Because she would be naked," Nico said with a smirk. "I don't care if we are like brothers, I don't think you want me to see your woman naked."

Phoenix narrowed his eyes at him and growled, "You're damn right I don't! Go look at your own mate."

Laughing again, Nico told him, "Trust me, I will." Ten minutes later the helicopter touched the ground a few yards away from RARE's plane and Jaxson went through the motions of shutting it down. Once everyone was out of the helicopter, Nico looked over at Phoenix with his eyebrows raised. "What do you have to take care of this chopper?"

"I got just the thing," Phoenix said nodding towards their plane. "In my bag in the back." Nico ran towards the jet to get the bag while Phoenix stood next to the chopper, his hand braced against it to hold him up. When Nico returned, Phoenix took his bag from him and pulled out one of his toys. He rigged the explosive to the side of the chopper, set the timer for 20 minutes, and with Nico's help made his way to the jet. Slowly they climbed up the stairs into the plane with Serenity following close behind, still in her wolf form.

Holy hell, Phoenix hurt. Nico lead him to the back of the plane where he had Phoenix lie down on the floor while he got out his first aid kit. Ripping Phoenix's jeans open above the knee, Nico carefully inspected the wound. "You're lucky, Phoenix," he said. "It's not in an artery. This is gonna hurt like a bitch though." That was all the warning Nico gave before he yanked the tin from Phoenix's leg. Phoenix let out a strangled gasp and passed out. Working quickly, Nico cleaned and stitched the wound, Serenity growling at him the whole time. She was one pissed off wolf. After he was done, Nico went over to Phoenix's bag and found Serenity a tee shirt.

"He is going to be fine, Serenity. Trust me," Nico said. "You might want to shift before the rest of the team shows up." Placing the shirt on the floor beside her, Nico turned and headed to the front of the plane to wait for his team.

Phoenix woke up to the most beautiful sound he had ever heard, Serenity's voice. "Wake up, Phoenix," she demanded softly. "Wake up for me, my sexy mate." He moaned and moved his head toward her voice. "I am here, Phoenix. I am here with you. Wake up and see me."

She trailed a hand down the side of his face and then traced the tattoo that ran down his neck. She ran her hand over his shoulder and down his arm, tracing the muscles as she went. He shivered at her touch, his cock immediately hardening. "Are you with me?" she asked him softly.

With her? Fuck yeah he was with her. As Phoenix opened his mouth to tell her just how with her he was, he heard other voices. He reached for his Glock, but she grabbed his arm before he could take it out of its holder. "It's ok. Your team just got here and we are getting ready to take off. We are safe now, Phoenix. Rest."

As Phoenix opened his eyes, pain sliced through his head. Crap, that wasn't good was it? He closed his eyes again on a groan. Shit, he probably did have a concussion. It fucking hurt.

"Shhh," he heard Serenity whisper. She reached up and placed one of her hands on his head and the other on his ribs. All of the sudden, sharp pain slammed through him. Crying out, his body arched up and then slammed back to the floor. What the fuck was going on? The pain was worsening; no it was lessening. What the fuck? How was that possible?

"No, Serenity, no!" Rikki yelled. "Phoenix would not want you to do that!" Do what? What was she doing? Phoenix tried to remain conscious, but it was a losing battle. Slipping into darkness, his last thought was of Serenity's beautiful brown eyes.

When Phoenix came to again, he gradually opened his eyes waiting for the blinding pain to hit him, only this time there was nothing. In confusion, he opened his eyes all the way and slowly looked around. Rikki was sitting beside him with Serenity's head in her lap. She was gently stroking Serenity's long dark hair out of her face. What the hell had happened? Moving carefully, Phoenix slowly sat up. The pain in his head was gone. His ribs were sore, but nothing like before. Even his leg felt a lot better.

"She healed you and took your pain," Rikki said as she continued stroking Serenity's hair. "She did the same for me when I was shot. After healing me, it took her four days to recover. I was afraid she wasn't going to make it. She was running a high fever and was so pale. And she would cry out in pain, her body trembling."

Phoenix looked at Serenity in horror. At her pale face, the shadows under her eyes, the grimace on her lips. She had taken his pain? How could she handle so much pain in her tiny body? Feeling groggy, but with the pain just a dull ache now, Phoenix scooted over next to Serenity. Reaching down, he gathered her up into his arms and held her close. Rocking her gently back and forth, he kissed her on the top of her head, her cheek, her pert little nose. She moaned softly as if in pain, and Phoenix snuggled her closer. He was supposed to be protecting her; instead, she was protecting him.

"Tell them to hurry the hell up," he growled at Rikki. "We need to get Serenity to Doc Josie now." Leaning back, Phoenix held Serenity close, talking to her the entire flight to Denver about anything and everything. She probably would not remember any of it. But it made him feel better and he was hoping that if she was conscious on some level, hearing his voice was making her feel better too.

Chapter 15

As soon as the jet touched down in Denver, everyone immediately gathered their gear and exited the plane moving towards the waiting SUVs. Driving pedal to the metal, they ended up at the White River wolves' compound in record time. When the SUV stopped in front of the hospital, Phoenix gathered Serenity in his arms and hit the ground running. She was still unconscious from healing Phoenix on the plane and he was scared to death. He had not just found his mate to lose her again. Oh, hell no. Phoenix yelled for Doc Josie, the doctor for the White River wolves, as he took the stairs two at a time. The minute he cleared the hospital entrance, Doc Josie was there. "Put her in the first room," she ordered and motioned for two nurses to follow her.

Phoenix gently laid Serenity on the bed, but refused to let go of her hand. "Talk to me, Phoenix," Doc Josie urged. "What the hell is going on?" Serenity moaned softly in pain, her eyes fluttering as though she was trying to open them. She was obviously hurting, but there was not a scratch or bruise on her.

Trying to soothe her, Phoenix gently smoothed back her hair. "She healed me. I was hurt badly, Doc, and she healed me with her ability. She took my pain. You have to do something," he pleaded. Serenity cried out loudly, her body folding into a tight ball. Sweat beaded on her forehead and she started panting. Phoenix reached out to run a hand down her leg and she screamed. Quickly drawing his hand back, he glared up at Doc Josie. "Do something, dammit," he demanded. "Help her."

The doctor looked at him with pity in her eyes. "I can't, Phoenix, I'm sorry. I have only come across something like this once before, and there wasn't anything we could do then either. When she healed you, she took all of your pain. While she may not look like she has your injuries, for all intents and purposes, she does. Wherever you were hurt, she is now hurt. Whatever you were feeling, she is now feeling. I could give her pain medicine, but past experience has proven because she is a shifter it would wear off extremely quickly. The most I can do is try and make her comfortable until the pain has subsided enough that she can shift and help speed the healing process."

"Why the hell did she do it? I've been hurt a lot worse. It would have taken awhile, but I would have been fine," Phoenix growled clenching his hands in fists. He wanted to touch Serenity, but was afraid. He didn't want to accidentally hurt her again.

"She did it because you are hers, Phoenix," Angel said from behind him. "Shifters will do anything for their mates. She couldn't stand to see you in pain. You are human, she is not. She probably thought it would be better if she were in pain for a couple of days instead of you being in pain for weeks. Once she is up to it, she can shift into her wolf and speed up the healing process. She will be fine in hours after shifting."

"It's going to take longer than a couple of days," Rikki said as she walked into the room. Going to the other side of the bed, she stood gazing at Serenity. Reaching out, Rikki gently ran her fingers through Serenity's hair. "She was out for four days after healing my gunshot wound. Phoenix had broken ribs, a concussion, and a leg laceration. I wouldn't be surprised if she was out for a week this time."

Phoenix let out an impressive growl for being human. "If she ever does anything like this again, I am so paddling her ass." When Serenity moaned again in pain, he took off his shoes and slowly climbed into bed with her. Pulling her over, he draped her across his chest. Slipping her leg up and over one of his, Serenity snuggled into his chest. Then she was out again. Phoenix prayed it was a healing sleep because he couldn't stand knowing she was in pain and it was all because of him.

"I'll check in on her in an hour," Doc Josie assured Phoenix as she moved towards the door. Stopping, she turned to Angel, delicately sniffing the air in confusion. Raising her eyebrows she said, "Congratulations, I think?" Angel just growled and stomped out of the room.

Rikki stood by the bed watching Serenity. Tears filled her eyes and she turned to leave. "Wait," Phoenix said reaching out and grabbing her hand. "Come here, honey." Pulling her down with one arm, he hugged her tightly. "I am so glad you are home, Rikki." Rikki returned the hug before quickly stepping back.

"I wouldn't be if it wasn't for Serenity," Rikki told him. Swallowing hard she looked him in the eye. "She saved my life, Phoenix. She saved my life, and because she did, the General knows about her ability. He is going to come for her. There is no way he is going to give up easily when she has a gift to heal like hers. And if he gets her, the bastard will run every test on her that he can to figure out how her ability works. He will push Serenity until he kills her. Look at her. She can't keep doing this."

"He is not going to get her," Phoenix promised. "And he is not going to get you again either." Running his hand gently down Serenity's back as she moved restlessly in her sleep, he leaned over and placed a soft kiss on her head. "That bastard is never touching my woman again," he vowed.

Out of the corner of his eye, Phoenix saw movement in the doorway. Jeremiah Black was hovering in the open door. Nodding to him, Phoenix invited him in with a flick of his wrist. "Thanks man; I appreciate everything you did for Serenity and Rikki. I owe you one. You need anything, you call me."

Jeremiah nodded back, his gaze on Rikki, drinking her in. Reaching out, he wrapped a long strand of her hair around his finger. "You okay?" he asked Rikki as he tugged on the curl gently and then slowly let the shiny dark hair slide free to fall softly on her shoulders. Phoenix watched in amusement as Rikki's eyes widened and she struggled to speak. Then she seemed to close down. Reaching over, she grasped Phoenix's hand in a tight grip and quickly letting go, she hurried out of the room without a backward glance.

Jeremiah's phone rang, and swearing under his breath, he walked over by the window to answer it. After a few minutes, he hung up and turned towards Phoenix, the frustration clear in his voice. "That was the office. We have a lead on a case I've been working. I need to go."

Phoenix looked at Jeremiah in surprise. "Aren't you going to tell Rikki that you're mates? I think she should know."

"Look," Jeremiah growled. "She's obviously still not ready. Before this happened, I was ready to pressure her into mating with me, but I have decided I am not going to push it. I don't want to lose her before anything even gets started. She means too much to me." He walked over to the door and then turned back. "Keep an eye on her for me, please?" he asked shoving his fingers through his dark hair.

Phoenix laughed. "She'd roast your balls on a stick if she knew you asked me that, man. You know she likes to think she can take care of herself. But yeah, I got your back."

Wistfully looking at the way Phoenix held his mate, Jeremiah turned and left the room. Phoenix sighed deeply. He did not know for sure what had happened to Rikki in her past, but he knew that she and Jeremiah had a difficult road ahead of them. After running away from foster care at 15, Rikki learned to rely only on herself. It was very hard for her to trust anyone. As far as Phoenix knew, Rikki had never been in any kind of a personal relationship. It was going to be interesting watching Rikki dance around Jeremiah, and he was going to sit back and enjoy the show. He just hoped there was a happily ever after for the two of them. He planned on making one for himself and Serenity.

Leaning down, he gave Serenity a kiss on the tip of her nose, and then he closed his own eyes and drifted off to sleep.

****

Standing near the back corner of the hospital, Rikki watched as Jeremiah Black walked out the door and moved towards where Jaxson stood talking to Nico by the SUV. Her heartbeat sped up as she traced his body with her eyes, from his thick brown hair, to his broad shoulders, down his back to the tight butt she wanted to reach out and squeeze. She was curious, was it as hard as it looked? Rikki wanted to go talk to him; she loved the low tones of his voice. But she was scared. Jeremiah made her feel things she had never felt. Every time he was around, she froze. Her body, her voice, her mind; everything froze. She felt off balance, and Rikki hated that feeling.

As she watched, Jeremiah said something to Jaxson, climbed into the back of the vehicle and slammed the SUV's door shut. Raising his eyebrows, Jaxson sent Nico a short wave. Moving around to the driver's side, Jaxson opened the door and slid behind the wheel. As he backed up, Jeremiah glanced over and found Rikki. When his eyes met hers, he lifted his hand and placed it on the window. Slowly, she lifted her hand and held it straight out, mimicking him. The last thing she saw was his sexy grin as Jaxson drove away.

Chapter 16

Angel was at a loss as to what to do. In one room, Trace was with Jade. Jade, the daughter Angel had not seen in too many years. The guilt Angel felt over not being able to find Jade, then discovering she had been the General's captive for the past 20 years, was excruciating. She had gone over the night Jade was taken numerous times in her mind, wondering what she could have done differently to change the final outcome. In her mind, it always turned out the same, but she could not stop punishing herself with the 'what if' scenarios. Angel was afraid to go into Jade's room to find out her daughter would never forgive her for not keeping her safe.

In another room, Serenity lay in bed suffering from healing Phoenix and absorbing his pain. Phoenix would be dealing with an intense sense of fear and probably self-condemnation. He would need someone from the team to be there with him and help him get a handle on his emotions so he could concentrate on Serenity. As much as Angel wanted to be there for Phoenix and Serenity, she did not want to be away from her daughter any longer.

Then there was the unresolved issue with Chase. Angel's wolf was pushing her to go find Chase and finish what she had started, but Angel was fighting it. The issue was that the mating bond was not complete yet, and it was killing her wolf to be apart from him. Until the bond was fully in place, she and Chase would both be in hell. Angel had really messed things up this time. She wanted to be near Chase, but she had fucked that up and had no idea how to fix it. Being near Chase would pacify her wolf, and Angel wanted to lean on him and soak in his calming presence. She was about to see her daughter for the second time in 20 years, and Angel did not want to do it alone. Her pride would not allow her to ask Chase for his help, though. She had been on her own for most of her life; she could handle this herself.

Without another thought, Angel made her way to Jade's room. Yes, she was definitely going to see her daughter before doing anything else. Angel was not going to be separated from Jade for another moment. Too much time had already passed.

Walking down the hall of the hospital, Angel stopped at the door to her daughter's room. There was no doubt in her mind that Jade was hers. She had held her every single night, rocking her to sleep and inhaling her scent, for four years. Jade had been her life, her reason for getting up every morning. She had lived to see the joy in Jade's beautiful green eyes, to see the dimples in her cheeks flash with her laughter. Angel had been searching for Jade ever since she had been taken 20 years ago, but everywhere she'd looked had been a dead end. No matter how hard she had tried, after that first year, she could no longer connect telepathically with Jade.

Now that Angel knew Jade had been the General's prisoner, she was sure he'd had something to do with her inability to connect with her daughter. It was too much of a coincidence that Angel had not been able to connect with Jade for the past 19 years and then she was unable to connect with Rikki after she was taken. She made a mental note to talk to her team about it later.

Pushing the door open, Angel quietly entered the room. The doctor was beside Jade's bed softly asking her questions and checking her vitals. Trace was standing with his back to them staring out the window. He did not turn around when Angel entered the room, but she figured it was because he was trying to give Jade some privacy.

Angel started towards her daughter, but stopped when Jade shook her head once and motioned toward Trace. Obviously, Jade wanted her to check on Trace instead. Walking to Trace, she stood quietly at his side and waited. She could feel the tension pouring off him. Angel thought about asking him to tell her what was wrong, but she knew with Trace you had to wait until he was ready to talk. Trace was a very private person. If he wanted you to know something, he would tell you. Otherwise, whatever was going on with him was off limits. Angel knew that part of that was his cat. They were solitary creatures. Being around a lot of people bothered him and he did not completely trust anyone. Another much bigger part of it was his past.

Angel knew some things about Trace's past. When she conducted the background check on him, she had gone far enough back to find out where he came from. Who he came from. Trace had a big target on his back. He was being hunted by a Columbian drug cartel. As though being hunted was not bad enough, the situation was much worse. The cartel's leader, Philip Perez, was Trace's own father. Because of this, Angel had known when she hired Trace that it could come back to bite her in the ass someday.

Trace had been groomed early in his life to take over the cartel. Unfortunately for Trace's father, Trace had been born with the morals that his father was lacking. While he had no problem pulling the trigger on some lowlife piece of shit who deserved it, there was no way he was killing innocents.

Trace left Columbia when he was 25 and had been on his own until he had hooked up with RARE. His father had refused to let him go, though, and continued sending his lackeys after him to try and either take him back or take him out. No one had gotten close enough to catch Trace yet, not that had lived to talk about it anyway. Angel even had a hand in eliminating a couple of them herself. She had never told Trace about the ones she took care of before they could get near him. He was a part of RARE, and RARE was her family. She took care of them. Not once had she regretted her decision to allow Trace to become a part of her family.

Angel also knew that Trace had a mother and a sister somewhere. From what she had figured out, when Trace had left the cartel, he had taken them and hidden them so that his father would never find them. That was probably the only reason his father wanted him alive if possible. He wanted to torture him until Trace gave up his family. Obviously, his father did not know Trace at all if he thought any amount of torture would make him turn on them.

Sometimes Trace would leave for a couple of weeks. When he came back, he would not talk for days. Normally Trace was not big on talking, but this was different. Angel had connected with him once when he was gone for a full month just to make sure he was still alive. It was the last time she had done it. She had felt so much emotional pain and despair that she had tried to reach out and comfort him through the link. He had slammed a wall up between them so fast that it had physically hurt her. They had not talked about it later, but from then on Angel had respected his privacy and trusted that he would return to them when he was able.

As far as Angel was aware, no one else on the team knew anything about his past, and she respected that. But, she had a feeling that his past was about to cause a problem with the present.

We need to talk, she heard him whisper into her mind.

Is she yours? Angel asked him. She was sure Jade was Trace's mate. She had never seen him act even remotely protective or possessive over anyone before. He cared about his team members, but he acted as if finding and saving others was just a job to him.

I need to leave, Trace said without answering her question. *I have some things I need to take care of so that the people I care about are safe.*

Angel did not respond right away. If he was Jade's mate and he was leaving her already, this was not going to go over very well. However, knowing what she knew about his past, she had a good idea as to what he was going to do. *When?* She asked.

Now. The sooner I get it handled, the sooner I can get back. It should take me two months tops. Looking over at Jade he demanded, *Take care of her while I'm gone, Angel.*

That was all Angel needed to hear. Trace had just confirmed her suspicions. Not once had he ever demanded anything of her. *I would ask you to take someone with you, but I already know what your response would be. Be safe, Trace. Check in with me if you can. And...come home soon. My daughter needs you. We need you.*

Trace walked over to Jade. She and the doctor were just finishing up. "She is doing well," Doc Josie said. "A little malnourished, but that is easily fixed. You take care of yourself, Jade. If you need anything, call or stop by. I am almost always here."

As Doc Josie left the room, Trace moved closer to Jade. Bending down he nuzzled her cheek and breathed in deeply. Cupping her face gently, he kissed her softly on the lips. "I have to go," he whispered. "I'm going to be gone for a few months, but I will be back for you. Stay with Angel. She will keep you safe for me."

Jade's beautiful dark green eyes filled with tears, but all she said was, "Be safe." After one last kiss, Trace left the room without a backwards glance.

"He is protecting you," Angel told Jade softly. "He will be back as soon as he can." Jade nodded but Angel knew she did not fully understand. If you asked Angel, having a mate was a huge pain in the ass. She had not even wanted one, and now she was mated to an alpha. Well, halfway mated, anyway.

"Hey," she said taking hold of Jade's hand, clutching it tightly as tears filled her eyes. "This will just give us a chance to get to know one another. I've missed you so much, Jade."

Taking a hold of Jade's chin and lifting her head so that she could look into her eyes, Angel told her, "I looked for you, Jade. I looked everywhere. You were just gone. I was devastated. You were my life. I wasn't sure I could go on without you, but I pushed forward. I pushed forward even when I couldn't connect with you. I still believed you were out there, somewhere. I never gave up on you."

Jade threw her arms around Angel and held on tightly sobbing. "I never forgot you either," she whispered. They sat like that for what seem like hours. Finally Angel pulled back and whispered, "Let's go home."

Chapter 17

Serenity was in so much pain. Her entire body ached, and she was afraid to move. Waking up like this was becoming a habit, a bad habit that she definitely needed to break. As Serenity tried to push through the pain, she struggled to remember what happened to put her in this condition. Before opening her eyes, she wanted to know what kind of shit storm she would be facing this time around. She prayed it was not as bad as the last one she had found herself in with the General when his minions had kidnapped her intending to use her in the breeding program.

As the pain pounded through her temples, Serenity slowly started to remember. The General had drugged her and taken her to a building out in the middle of the desert. Rikki, a woman who had been a part of the group that had tried to rescue her originally, had been shot. Serenity had used her special abilities to take Rikki's pain and heal her. That was how she had ended up in the same situation last time that she was in now. She'd had Rikki to protect her then, but who was going to protect her now?

Squeezing her eyes tightly shut, Serenity tried to remember what had happened after that. Her mind was sluggish and her head was pounding, making it difficult to remember anything. What the hell had happened to her to make her feel like this?

She remembered running through the halls of the building where she and Rikki were held, shooting a guard, then she was outside. Jade was held in a deep hole at the back of the building. Serenity remembered a huge black panther prowling around the opening of the hole and then it jumped in after Jade. Why in the hell was a black panther in a desert in the middle of nowhere? There had been other people around, people Rikki had known and trusted. Then Jade was out of the hole and there was the sound of a helicopter heading toward them. Everyone was running, and a building blew apart. Phoenix! Screaming his name, Serenity's eyes flew open and she sat up in the bed quickly, falling back down as waves of pain slammed through her. She felt hands on her, gently stroking her hair. A face was down by hers, nuzzling her neck. A deep voice whispered, "I'm here, Beauty. I am right here. You are safe." Inhaling deeply, she breathed in her mate's scent as she lost consciousness again.

The next time Serenity woke, she recognized Phoenix's scent right away. She was not afraid to open her eyes. Her mate was there and he would protect her. Looking around the room, she spotted him asleep in the corner. Phoenix was lounging back with one leg thrown up over the arm of the chair, his head tilted to the side. Serenity could just barely see the tempting tattoo that ran up the back of his neck. Licking her lips, she thought about how she wanted to trace that tattoo, along with all of the other ones on his body, with her tongue. She knew he had a tattoo on his chest that normally showed just above his tee shirt, but with the way he was positioned in the chair, she could not see it. However, she loved the beautiful intricate design running down his left arm.

Phoenix held a notebook in one hand and what looked like a charcoal pencil in the other. He had obviously fallen asleep while sketching something, but she could not see what. Eagerly, Serenity drank him in with her eyes. He was the sexiest thing she had ever seen, and he was all hers. She wondered how long she had been out. He looked exhausted.

Slowly, Serenity closed her eyes again and concentrated on her injuries. She was still in pain, but it was not as bad as the last time she had woken. She needed to shift. She would be as good as new if she became her wolf for a few hours. As far as Serenity could tell by the scents in the air and background noise, she was in a hospital. If she concentrated, she could hear voices beyond her door. Definitely doctors, not scientists. Was it a hospital for humans or a hospital for shifters?

Serenity decided she was beyond giving a shit at this point. Slowly she got out of bed and made her way to use the restroom. When she was done, she painfully made her way back to the bed. A quick glance at Phoenix proved he was still asleep, so she removed her clothes and within moments a small black wolf stood where she had been. Much better. The pain was almost gone now.

Glancing at the bed, Serenity decided there was another place she would much rather be. Moving toward Phoenix she leaped into his lap, knocking the notebook and charcoal pencil to the floor. His eyes sprang open as his arms wrapped around her. A low rumbling noise similar to a purr came out of her throat as she snuggled up into him. As Phoenix gently stroked her fur, Serenity fell into a deep healing sleep.

Chapter 18

Phoenix picked Serenity up and moved to the bed. Laying her down, he settled in beside her. He pulled her over until most of her body was lying across his chest. Serenity had shifted into her wolf, and he knew that meant she would heal faster than normal. Stroking her fur, Phoenix thought about the amount of trust that she was placing in him, and it shocked the hell out of him. The only thing Phoenix knew about Serenity's past was the General had held her for who knew how long. He did not know what road she had travelled that had brought her to the General's attention. Just the fact that she had been with the General at all would make one think that was enough to kill the trust any woman would have in anyone ever again. Here she was, though, fast asleep in her wolf form on his chest, trusting him to protect her. It was enough to bring tears to his eyes. Wiping them away quickly, he sank his fingers into the fur on Serenity's neck, his other hand going to the gun at his side. He would guard her with his life. No one was getting near his woman again.

The door opened and Doc Josie walked in. Her face lit up at the sight of Serenity asleep in her wolf form. "Perfect!" she said. "She will be good as new when she wakes up." She stopped moving when she saw Phoenix palming his Glock. Glancing once more at Serenity, she held her hands up in a calming manner. Smiling at Phoenix, she took a couple of steps back. "When she wakes up, you can take her home, Phoenix." With another quick grin, the doctor turned and left.

Phoenix knew he was being unreasonable. Doc Josie was just checking on Serenity because she was her patient. But it didn't matter. He did not give a shit what anyone thought, no one was getting near his mate. No one. Tightening the hand in her fur, he kept his other hand on his Glock.

A couple of hours later, Phoenix heard Serenity let out a sigh as she stretched against him. He glanced down into her beautiful eyes, and in the next instant he had his arms full of hot, beautiful woman. Oh fuck, he thought as his cock instantly grew rock hard in his jeans. There was no way she could miss it. One of his arms was in her long dark hair, cupping the back of her head. The other was holding onto her nice, soft ass.

Unable to stop himself, he pushed his hips up into her, groaning loudly. Her nostrils flared and her eyes turned wolf, a low growl vibrating in her throat. Serenity moved up and straddled him, her hot core on his pulsing cock. Grinding against him, she leaned in and nuzzled his neck, flicking her tongue out and slowly dragging it up towards his ear. Phoenix felt her hand moving down his chest and then lower until it stroked over his dick. Holy shit, if she didn't stop he was going to come in his pants. He wanted to take Serenity right there. To shove himself deep inside of her and make her scream his name loudly as she flew apart. But he refused to take her for the first time in a hospital room with staff right outside the door. He was not above the whole making her fly apart a couple of times thing, though. This was going to be all about her.

Groaning, Phoenix tried to move her hand away and was surprised to hear the warning growl from her throat as she clamped her teeth down on his shoulder. Not hard enough to break the skin, but hard enough to let him know that she was beyond control right now. "Wait, baby," he ground out. She growled louder, biting down harder.

Phoenix wanted nothing more than to be fully mated with Serenity, but now was not the time. Phoenix wanted to get to know her first. Find out what she liked and disliked. This was his mate, not some random fuck. He wanted to share everything about himself with her before they took that final step-from his time in foster care, to being in the military, and finally finding RARE. The good, the bad and the ugly, as they say. Hell, she should get a chance to back out of she wanted.

Acting quickly, Phoenix wrapped one of his legs around one of hers, tightened his arms around her and flipped her underneath him. Serenity's head flung back and her eyes widened in surprise. "I have ya, my Beauty," he whispered.

Bending his head, Phoenix closed the distance between them and claimed her mouth in a demanding kiss. He tried to slow down because this was for Serenity, not him, but he couldn't. He had to taste her, had to touch her. Slipping past Serenity's lips as she gasped in pleasure, he tangled his tongue with hers. Slowly he slid a hand down to cup one of her full breasts, gently flicking the nipple. Serenity cried out as she yanked her lips away. She tried to reach down and grab him again, but he stopped her. "This is for you, Beauty," he growled.

Taking both of her arms, he pulled them above her head and grasped them in his hand. "Now, where was I?" he growled, leaning over and nibbling down her neck to her breast. Cupping it again in his other hand, he flicked his tongue out and licked her nipple. Serenity arched into his mouth, moaning loudly.

Phoenix continued licking and sucking on her nipple as he moved his hand across her hip and over until he was stroking her. "Oh God," she cried out as he slowly slipped one finger inside of her. Using his thumb, he rubbed her clit, while slowly adding another finger, moving both in and out of her moist heat. As Phoenix bit down lightly on her nipple, Serenity came while screaming his name. They definitely were not hiding what just happened from anyone in the hospital. Good, he thought. Everyone would know Serenity was his.

Phoenix leaned over and lightly kissed Serenity on the lips, but moved back when she tried to deepen it. "Not here," he told her, leaning his forehead on hers. "As much as I love that the entire hospital knows you are mine, I don't want our first time to be here."

Breathing heavily, Serenity wrapped her arms around Phoenix and held on, digging her nails into his back. "I need more, Phoenix," she moaned. "Please, give me more."

Raising his eyebrows, he kissed her and then slowly slipped down her body, trailing kisses on the way. When he reached his destination, he glanced up with a wicked grin. "Is this what you need?" he asked. Serenity moaned and lifted her hips up to his mouth again. "Please," she gasped.

Grasping Serenity's hips and holding her down, Phoenix leaned in and licked her clit. "Yes," she cried out as she tried to move her hips up towards him again. He just chuckled, and tightening his hold on her, he flicked his tongue out again. Panting loudly, Serenity grabbed hold of his head and pushed him down. Phoenix laughed and then got busy. In no time, Serenity was coming again and Phoenix was on his way to having blue balls. Pulling back with one last lick, Phoenix moved back up until he was face to face with Serenity. "Better?" he smirked.

"For now," she purred leaning back into the pillow with a fully satisfied smile on her face. Laughing, Phoenix got up and entered the bathroom. He debated on taking care of himself, but Serenity would know, and he did not want to upset her. When Serenity had tried to touch him, he had told her what they were doing was for her. So instead Phoenix chose to walk around in pain, praying his hard on would go away, but knowing that it would not anytime soon.

Exiting the bathroom, he walked over to the closet, where he pulled out his bag and set it on the foot of the bed. "You wanna get out of here?" he asked, praying she would be okay leaving with him. It was just going to be the two of them right now, he did not care about anyone else. He wanted to be alone with Serenity. "Nico's mate, Jenna, dropped off some clothes for you to wear. They should work until we can go shopping."

"Really? Just like that?" Serenity asked with a hopeful look on her face. He pulled some clothes out of his bag and tossed them to her. Excitedly jumping out of bed, Serenity turned away from Phoenix to put the clothes on. That's when Phoenix got the first glimpse of her tattoo. "Wait," he told her as he stared at her back in stunned silence. She looked over her shoulder at him, but did not say a word when she saw where he was looking. She pulled her hair up over her shoulder and bowed her head. Covering most of Serenity's back was the most beautiful tattoo Phoenix had ever seen. It was a tattoo of a brightly colored phoenix in orange, red, yellow and blue. The artist that had put it on her was a rock star. Phoenix was a bit jealous. He didn't think he could have drawn a better one if he tried. Reaching out, he traced the tattoo from the top of its head down to the last feather that flowed right above her tailbone. Absolutely magnificent.

Turning her to face him, Phoenix reached up and removed the phoenix necklace from around his neck and put it on Serenity. "So beautiful," he whispered. "Mine."

Serenity smiled up at him and pulled him in for a quick kiss. Not bothering to turn around for privacy, she started dressing. The jeans were a bit big around the waist and the hot pink tee shirt was snug in the chest, but Phoenix thought she was sexy as hell. He didn't know how long he was going to be able to keep his no-sex-until-he-got-to-know-her-better rule. Hopefully, at least until he got her home. Then two thoughts entered his lust-filled mind. First, he probably should not take her back to the condo. It might not be safe. The second was Hunter. He hated to disappoint Serenity when she looked so excited, but he could not just leave the compound without checking on Hunter.

A few weeks ago RARE raided a facility in Mexico that was holding two women and three children. Hunter, a young bear shifter, had attached to Phoenix right away and had become his little sidekick until Phoenix found out about Serenity. At that moment, he had basically forgotten about Hunter. He needed to check on him before he would be able to concentrate on his mate.

Slipping his arms around Serenity, he quietly explained Hunter to her. "I have to go see him, Beauty. I'm sorry, but I feel like I have neglected him. He trusted me and I let him down."

Reaching up, Serenity trailed a hand from the top of his head down to cup his cheek. "You are the sweetest badass I have ever met, Phoenix...what is your last name?"

He burst out laughing. "Madison," he told her. "Phoenix Madison."

She blushed and smacked him lightly on the arm. "Well, when have I had a chance to ask that question?"

"What's yours?" Phoenix asked still laughing. Serenity grew quiet and stepped back. Turning away, she grabbed Phoenix's bag and turned to leave. "We better go check on Hunter before you lose hero status," she said over her shoulder as she walked out. Phoenix stood watching her walk away, but decided to just go with it for now. He would talk to her later when they were alone, and she would tell him what was going on. He would prove to her that she could trust him. No one was ever going to harm her again. Phoenix would protect her from anyone and anything; he would *always* be there for her.

Chapter 19

Serenity wanted to kick herself. She had no idea why she had acted like that with Phoenix. She had no reason not to trust him; but old habits die hard. Serenity had been running for so long, that she did not know how to stop. She almost gave him the last name she had been using when the General kidnapped her, but she could not lie to Phoenix. She would not have a relationship based on lies.

Stopping at the hospital exit, Serenity waited for Phoenix to catch up with her. "Campbell," she whispered to him as he stood beside her. "My last name is Campbell."

Phoenix grasped her hand, kissing her knuckles. "Now it's Madison," was all he said. Smiling shyly, Serenity peered up at him between the hair that had fallen forward to cover her face. "Serenity Madison. It has a nice ring to it." He placed a kiss on the top of her head, hugging her closely. Smiling, they turned as one and walked out into the sunshine.

Serenity loved to be outside, but the General had never allowed it. Not only were the women required to stay inside the building; they were rarely allowed to leave their room. Feeling the sun on her face was heaven. To walk out, feel the sun shining down on her, and know that she was free was one of the best feelings in the world. Serenity was oblivious to the slight chill in the air. To her, the day, the weather, it was perfect.

"I've been staying with my friend Nico and his mate Jenna," Phoenix said, "But I have a condo in town where we can stay for privacy. I'm going to be honest with you, though, I don't feel comfortable taking you out of the compound. As much as I want to take you home with me, I have a feeling this is not over. The General is going to come after you and Jade."

"You want to leave me here?" whispered Serenity, the distress obvious in her voice. Phoenix looked at her in confusion. "Why would I leave you here? I'm staying with you, Serenity. Where you are, I am with you. We just need to figure out where that is going to be."

Serenity took a deep breath. What was wrong with her? Of course he wasn't going to leave her. She was his mate and he took that seriously. She knew that, but for a second her insecurities surfaced and she worried Phoenix was going to leave her at the compound. Leave her alone to fend for herself and that scared her. Wait, Phoenix kept mentioning the compound. What was the compound anyway? Serenity had quite a few questions, but those would have to wait. They had a little boy to see first.

Phoenix reached out and took his bag from her grasp, throwing it over one of his wide shoulders. Reaching down he grabbed her hand and tugged her down the stairs and through the hospital gardens. Serenity breathed in deeply as they walked. There were so many different smells in the air, but her favorite one was the scent of her mate.

Taking another deep breath, she held his scent inside her as long as she could. Finally she had to exhale. She saw the looks Phoenix was getting and it was pissing her off. Her wolf wanted her to grab him and mark him. To show all the bitches walking around the compound that he was hers and they should back off. However, Serenity knew all of his attention was on her. His gaze had not strayed. That soothed her wolf somewhat, and put a smile on Serenity's face.

Soon, she would claim Phoenix, and everyone would know he was hers. There was just a little biting and a lot of sex that needed to happen first, then it would become official. She was claiming her mate tonight, and they were not going to be quiet about it. There was no way they could stay at Nico's and Jenna's with Hunter there.

Walking up the sidewalk to the small cottage style house, Serenity tried to think of a plan. They could not stay here, but they could not go to Phoenix's condo. She had no idea where they were now. And seriously, what the hell was the compound? Why did they call it that? It sounded like one of those cult places where people went and drank the red Kool Aid to die. Maybe she should get answers to some of her questions sooner rather than later.

Serenity was starting to become anxious when she felt a hand on her back. Phoenix leaned in and softly told her, "I'm going to text Chase and see if, maybe, he has an apartment we can stay in until everything with the General is handled. Something here at the compound. It will give us some privacy, and you will be safe."

"As long as we don't have to wear white robes and drink red Kool Aid, I'm good," Serenity told him. She laughed nervously as Phoenix looked at her in confusion. "You keep calling this place a compound. That makes me nervous, Phoenix. More than nervous, freaked out really."

Phoenix burst out laughing. "Awe, baby, you are so adorable," he said. "That's just what the White River Wolves call this place. It's their home. They have had threats in the past, so Chase's dad put a huge fence around an extensive amount of their land. The pack has more enforcers and trackers than a normal pack would have to cover any issues or threats. The hierarchy is basically the same as any other wolf pack; they just have more force behind it because the safety of the pack means everything to Chase, the current Alpha. When Chase's parents died, he made very few changes. He kept things the way they are because it works."

Embarrassed, Serenity looked down and shrugged. "Well what was I supposed to think? A compound to me is either a place where people are being held against their will, which obviously isn't the case here, or some kind of fanatic religious group who follow a leader claiming to be a higher power. That always turns out bad."

Still laughing, Phoenix pulled Serenity into his arms. "I promise, no one is here against their will and Chase isn't going to make you drink anything you don't want to. You can trust me, Serenity. I am not going to let anything happen to you."

Just then the door flew open and a little dark haired boy threw himself into Phoenix's arms. Phoenix picked him up and the child sniffled as he wrapped his arms around Phoenix's neck tightly. Well, shit, Serenity thought. So much for claiming her mate tonight. They were not going anywhere.

Chapter 20

The General sat at his desk in his remote Alaskan facility. It was in the middle of nowhere and was cold as hell, but there was also a slim to none chance RARE would even think of looking for him there. He was trying to decide what he was going to do next. That disgusting team of mercenaries was not going to be allowed to sabotage the plans he had put into effect over 20 years ago. Because of them, he'd already moved all of his original facilities. Several women and their children, not to mention close to 75 of his own men, had been lost. His army was seriously depleted. He was working on getting that number back up now, but in the meantime he had no choice but to hide out in this god forsaken place.

The General refused to allow this to go on. This band of misfits was not going to ruin his plans. He had not sunk all of his time and money, let alone his reputation, into this project just to have RARE ruin him in less than a month. It had taken over 20 fucking years of his life to get this far. He was not giving up.

RARE could keep the women and brats they managed to rescue in the raids. He didn't give a shit about them. But, Serenity, he wanted Serenity back. The little bitch had been hiding her healing ability from him. The General sent a team of men to monitor her for months before they had finally grabbed her. Even though she refused to shift into wolf form in front of him, he had known she was a wolf shifter, but he hadn't known about her healing ability. The General wanted that ability. He wanted her back and wanted her studied by his scientists. And then he was going to find the perfect man to breed her with because he wanted children with her healing ability. It would be a huge benefit to his army. If injured, they could be healed quickly and sent right back into the action. Yes, that ability would be his.

The General wanted Jade back, too. But he wanted Jade for different reasons. At first, he had stolen Jade because he assumed she had the same abilities as her mother. Yeah, he knew who her mother was. He had known all along. The General was the one that had sent Jade's father to Angel in the first place. Angel had thought the man loved her. Unfortunately for Jade's father, he actually had come to care for Angel eventually and had refused to see reason where she was concerned. The General had made sure that problem was eliminated. The man had been one of his best soldiers; it had been a huge loss when he'd been taken out. But it was all for the greater good.

The General had originally wanted Angel, but he had known that Angel would be a huge pain in the ass and would fight him every step of the way. So instead of stealing her, he had manipulated the situation by placing one of his highly trained men into her life and getting her pregnant. Then he had stolen her children instead.

Angel had been pregnant with twins, a girl and a boy. She'd had no idea that when Jade was born, Jade's brother had lived. Angel thought that he had been stillborn. She was so devastated at the time that she hadn't questioned the doctors. Her son had lived, and that was the first child of Angel's the General had stolen. Four years later he had taken Jade.

Angel had no idea how the General had been manipulating events in her life all of those years ago. He thought it was funny how the events were playing out. Angel gets called in to save a child, only to find out that the General had also stolen her own child. Just wait until she found out her son, Jinx was still alive.

Yeah, the General wanted Jade back. He needed her back. It was the only way he could control her brother. He had been able to manipulate Jinx at a young age by threatening his sister, and the General had used that knowledge against him for several years. For some reason, the boy loved his sister, even though he had only met her twice. Once when he was four, and again when he was six after trying to rebel. The General had shown him what would happen to Jade if he tried it again.

Jinx was a cocky little shit, but he was good at what he did, which was basically whatever the General told him to do if he wanted Jade to live. Jinx had abilities he inherited from his father, along with his mother's abilities as well. Jinx was a wolf shifter, but he was so much more. The General needed him for the war that was coming. And that meant that he had to get Jade back, because without her there would be no controlling Jinx. There was not much the General was afraid of, but Jinx scared the hell out of him.

Picking up his phone, he made a call. By the time it was over, he was positive Jade and Serenity would be found and brought to him. And if he was lucky, he would get Angel as well.

Chapter 21

While Serenity and Jenna were getting dinner ready, Phoenix and Nico went out back to have a cold beer and talk. Lily and Hunter were playing on the swing set, but Hunter refused to go far from Phoenix. Phoenix hadn't realized how his staying away had affected Hunter. He had figured that Hunter would integrate himself into Nico's and Jenna's family and be happy. He had been so wrong.

Serenity had connected telepathically with Phoenix when he went outside and was not ashamed to admit that she was listening in on his and Nico's conversation. She was not ready to be away from Phoenix in any way right now. She needed to hold him close to her somehow, so she had connected to him without asking permission first. She hoped it would not piss him off, but she couldn't help herself.

"He cries at night," Nico told Phoenix as they watched the children. "He cries himself to sleep and then shifts into his bear form. It's hard to get him back out of it in the morning. Hunter doesn't feel safe when you aren't around, Phoenix."

Crap, Phoenix thought. There was no way he could leave the little guy tonight. He didn't want to upset Serenity, but Hunter needed him. *Stop worrying, Phoenix,* Serenity whispered into his mind. *We will stay here with Hunter or he will go where ever we go. We cannot leave him. We will not.*

Closing his eyes, Phoenix soaked in the intimate sound of Serenity's voice in his head. He felt connected to her in a way he had never felt with another woman. *Ask Nico if we can all stay here until the Alpha can find somewhere else for us. Preferably a two bedroom because Hunter will be coming with us.*

Smiling at the command in her voice, he looked back over at Nico who seemed to be waiting for a response from him. "Sorry, man, Serenity was talking to me. You mind if we hang here until Chase can find a place for us? I don't want to take Serenity back to the condo until I know it is safe. The General is going to be looking for her, but there's something else going on, too. I don't have the specifics yet, but I think someone else is after her besides the General."

"No worries, brother. You got a place here as long as you need one. We can move Hunter out to the couch so you and Serenity have some privacy. He can have the room back when Chase finds you a place."

"That's not necessary," Serenity said as she walked out the sliding glass door and made her way to Phoenix. "Hunter can stay in our room with us and when we leave, he will be coming with." There was no room for argument in her voice.

The surprise was evident on Nico's face. "Are you sure? He is more than welcome to stay here until the council decides where to send him."

"The council doesn't need to worry about Hunter anymore," Serenity told him. "You tell them that he is ours. His home is with us."

"Serenity," Phoenix warned her, "We don't get to make those decisions. We can request it, but with neither of us being bear shifters, they might not approve it."

"Bullshit," Serenity growled. "I am sure all of you have connections. Use them. That boy is staying with us, end of story. They do not want to fight me on this. They have no idea what I am capable of."

A small voice interrupted their conversation. "I can stay with you?" All eyes turned to the little boy that had made his way over without anyone noticing. Hunter was watching Serenity closely as he moved slowly towards her.

"You better believe it," she told him. "I'm not going to let anyone take you from us, Hunter. You belong with Phoenix and me."

"Yes, he does," Lily told them. "Hunter is your son now. The council will approve it." Serenity turned her gaze to the little girl who seemed so much older than her actual age. This was Jenna's daughter. Phoenix had told her about Lily. The General was after Lily, also. He had kidnapped her once, but RARE had rescued her.

Now Lily was watched very closely so nothing similar happened again. Lily was very gifted. Not only was she telepathic, but she also caught glimpses of the future. She had obviously seen Hunter with Phoenix and Serenity as a family in the future. Good, because even though she had just met Hunter, Serenity refused to give him up. Her mama wolf instincts had risen to the surface the moment she had seen him and no one was taking him from her. She knew it was not fair to try and hold on so tightly to Phoenix and Hunter when she had people trying to track her down to either kidnap or kill her, but Serenity refused to give them up. She would fight for them and she would win, dammit. They were hers.

Reaching out, Serenity gently ran her fingers through Hunter's curly brown hair. "Go play, Hunter," she told him. "I promise, we are not going to leave you. And no one is going to take you from us." Grinning widely, the child gave her a quick hug and tore off towards the swing set, Lily giggling and running behind him.

As Serenity watched Hunter go down the slide, Nico got down to business. "Serenity, Phoenix thinks someone besides the General is after you. Is there?"

"Shut the fuck up, Nico," Phoenix growled at him. "I will talk to her about it later."

"We need to know what kind of trouble she's in, Phoenix. We can't keep her safe if we don't know what we are up against. Not only that, but I need to be able to protect my family"

Serenity gasped. She hadn't even thought about the danger that was following her affecting Phoenix or his friends. She had been alone for so long. Why hadn't she thought about that? Malcolm had even gone so far as to kill her parents. And even though he hadn't tried to connect telepathically with her since she had shot him, she did not fool herself into thinking she was safe. No, that bastard would never stop coming after her until he either caught her or he was dead.

Serenity's eyes filled with tears. Just five minutes ago she had been fiercely thinking she would fight for Phoenix and Hunter, now she was wondering if she should go on the run again. If she left, then the bastards that were following her would not hurt anyone she cared about.

"Don't you even fucking think about it," Phoenix growled at her. "You aren't going anywhere. I went through hell knowing you were kidnapped by the General. We spent days trying to find you. Then I spent days by your bedside while you were in pain. I did not go through all of that just to have you run from me."

Phoenix was right. What was wrong with her? Yes, she had run for years from her past. But that was because there had been no one to turn to for help. Now she had a mate who cared about her, and he had RARE. One of the most elite mercenary teams out there. If they could not protect her, then no one could. And Serenity was not the spineless coward she had been. She was not going to leave Phoenix and Hunter. If Malcolm came after her again, she would make sure she killed him this time.

Phoenix reached out and pulled her down onto his lap. "You can't leave me, Beauty. If you do, then you will just have one more person hunting you because I refuse to let you go." Serenity snuggled into him, wrapping her arms around his neck and inhaling his scent. It soothed her wolf and calmed Serenity. As Phoenix held her, Serenity thought back to how it had all started. Sensing Jenna behind her, she motioned her over and began to tell her story.

"When I was eight years old, I was climbing trees with a friend of mine. She fell and broke her arm. She was in so much pain and I couldn't stand to see her cry. Someone ran to get the pack healer, but something made me go over to my friend and touch her arm where the break was.

I felt this heat, this power, flow through me and then it was like it jumped from my hand to her arm. She screamed and screamed, but I didn't let go. I had no idea what was happening. I was in so much pain, but this instinct made me hold onto her until I finally passed out.

When I came to, my mom told me about my great grandmother and her healing ability. It was passed down through the family, but Mom was hoping it would skip me since she did not have it. None of her sisters had gotten it, nor had her mother. She was hoping it was somehow gone.

When the pack healer saw what I could do, she went to the alpha and told him I needed to train under her. She wanted me there to heal everyone that she couldn't." Serenity paused as she remembered all of the pain she had gone through. She had suffered severely at the hands of her pack and no one except her parents had cared. As long as Serenity was able to heal the enforcers they weren't concerned about what it cost her.

"At first she just made me heal the people that had minor cuts. She wanted to see what I could do. Gradually she moved up to having me heal broken bones, knife wounds, things like that. I trained under her until I was 16. The older she got, the less she did, and the more I was required to heal. Finally I couldn't take it anymore. I was in constant pain and scared to death to go to her home every day to continue my training. One day, I packed a bag and without telling my parents, I ran."

Serenity got up and started pacing. That had been the easy part of her story. The next part really sucked. "I didn't know it, but the alpha's son had been watching me for years. I had always stayed clear of him because he was a sadistic son of a bitch that liked to take his anger out on people. Many of the broken bones I healed were because of him. Malcolm had the ability to connect with people like Angel and I do. Except he was an ass. He would make people do whatever he wanted by using his gift. When he found out I was gone, he went crazy. I had only made it about five miles when I felt him slam into my head with a force that scared the hell out of me. I tried to block him, but he ripped my control away so fast there wasn't anything I could do. I turned back around and walked the five miles back home with him inside my head the whole time. I fought and fought to kick him out, but he wouldn't budge. When I was finally back on pack lands, Malcolm was there to meet me."

Pausing, Serenity looked straight into Phoenix's eyes. Gathering her courage, she whispered, "I fought him as hard as I could, but the bastard not only mind raped me, he beat the hell out of me right there in front of everyone. No one stopped him because he claimed I was his mate and he was teaching me a lesson. He ripped the clothes from my body. I thought he was going to rape me, but he just wanted to humiliate me. He grabbed my breasts and twisted and squeezed them hard leaving large bruises. I had a broken arm and several bloody gashes all over my body.

My parents were locked in their house with several guards. There was nothing they could do. After it was over, Malcolm had a couple of the enforcers take me home. I was to get cleaned up and pack my bags. He said he would be back for me in a couple of days to move me in with him, but that he was leaving that night for a meeting."

Turning away from Phoenix, Serenity gazed at the darkening sky as she clenched her fists tightly. "My parents already had our bags packed when I got there. We left in the middle of the night with the help of one of the enforcers who did not agree with what Malcolm had done. I learned later Malcolm found out and had the enforcer killed. We ran for several years never letting ourselves stay in one place for too long. My gift to connect with people hadn't been my strongest gift when I was younger, but I practiced and practiced until I was strong enough to keep Malcolm out of my head."

Sitting back down beside Phoenix, Serenity rested her head on his shoulder as he slipped an arm round her, silently waiting for her to continue. "He caught up with us five years ago," she finally whispered. "We had been staying in a little cabin in a forest in Maine and we'd started feeling safe. Malcolm hadn't tried connecting with me for months. I even had a job. I was out meeting people, making a life for myself. One day I came home, and he was there. My parents were on the floor dead, and Malcolm stood over their bodies laughing at me.

There was blood all over the place. All over them, all over the floor, all over Malcolm. He had gone crazy. I didn't think twice. I pulled out the gun my dad had insisted I carry and shot the bastard. I unloaded the clip in him and then I turned and ran. Obviously I should have shot him in the head, though, because he lived. Every once in a while I feel him testing me, seeing how strong my shields are. He's still out there somewhere. I have no idea where."

Phoenix tightened his arms around Serenity as they sat in stunned silence. "Well shit," Nico said. "So you got not only the General on your ass, but you have a lunatic from your old pack, too." Glancing at Phoenix, Nico grinned suddenly. "I say we go after Malcolm first. Let's pull RARE together, hunt him down and eliminate him."

"I'm going to fucking kill him slowly," Phoenix growled. "He is going to wish he never touched what's mine. Call them, Nico. We're going hunting."

"Now wait just a minute, Phoenix," Serenity protested when Nico took out his phone. "You can't just go after Malcolm. First of all, you have no idea where he is. Second of all, he is crazy! And he can make you do things with his gift. He can make you hurt yourself and you won't be able to fight it."

"What he has isn't a gift, Serenity," Jenna said. "It is only a gift if you choose to help people with it. You never harm. What he has is a curse."

"We are going to find him, Serenity, and we are going to remove him from your life once and for all," Phoenix vowed. "And then we are going to go after the General and bring him down." Serenity did not know what to say. As much as she wanted to be free of Malcolm and her old pack, she didn't want to place anyone else in danger. As she tried to figure out a way to make everyone stand down, Nico ended his call.

"Angel will be here at 9am tomorrow. She is going to bring the team with so we can come up with a plan. You are family, Serenity. And we protect our family. Jenna, Angel wants you to call Chase and let him know about the meeting. It is up to him whether or not he comes, but as the White River Alpha, he deserves to know what's happening on his turf."

As Jenna nodded and walked off to make the call, Serenity looked at Phoenix and Nico in amazement. "Thank you," she whispered softly. "Thank you so much." Snuggling back into Phoenix, she clung to him as tears slipped down her cheeks. She had never thought that she might really be free of Malcolm someday. Serenity had accepted the fact that she might always be running from him. Now she had real hope that freedom was near. Well, freedom from Malcolm anyway. She would worry about the General another day.

Chapter 22

That night Hunter surprised everyone by insisting he wanted to have a sleepover in Lily's room. They made up a bed for him on her floor; the children were so tired they fell asleep within minutes.

While Serenity was getting ready for bed, Phoenix went to check with the enforcers guarding the perimeter around Nico and Jenna's home. When Phoenix was done, he made his way down the hall to the room he and Serenity would share. Opening the door, he quietly slipped inside. Gazing at Serenity snuggled under the covers, he silently shut the door. When he noticed her shoulders were bare and peeking out from under the comforter, Phoenix groaned. Bare, beautiful shoulders...wait, there were no straps of any kind. Holy shit, was she naked? "Serenity?" he questioned softly.

"Come here, Phoenix," Serenity demanded. "I'm tired of waiting. I need my mate." Phoenix's breath caught in his chest as she pushed the covers down past her chest. Her bare chest with the full perfect breasts that fit perfectly in his hands. The nipples that he loved to tease with his tongue and suck into his mouth. "I want to see you, Phoenix," she moaned as she reached up and cupped her own breasts, playing with the nipples. The phoenix necklace lay between them and it was like she was wearing his mark. It was hot as hell!

Phoenix shrugged his shirt off and started undoing the button on his jeans as he moved towards Serenity. "No briefs?" she teased as he slid down the zipper and slipped the pants off. Phoenix shook his head. "Too constricting," he ground out before he reached down and ripped the covers off the bed. As Serenity's eyes widened, Phoenix was on the bed and covering her with his body within seconds. Leaning down, he slowly traced her lips with his tongue and pushed his way inside her mouth. She tasted like fucking heaven.

Growling, Serenity reached up and raked her nails down his back. Phoenix pulled back when he felt her fangs graze his lips. Serenity watched him though eyes that had gone pure wolf. There was no way she was going to wait for foreplay.

Serenity pushed him over onto his back and straddled him. Reaching down, she grabbed hold of his cock and stroked once, twice. Oh shit, Phoenix thought, this was going to be fast. Serenity rose up on her knees and slid his cock into her hot, wet heat, slowly pushing down on top of him. "Mine," she growled. "Mine." Then she started moving, slowly at first and then faster and faster.

Jesus, he wasn't going to last. He could feel his orgasm building. "Mine," she growled again. Grabbing a hand full of her hair, he yanked her mouth to his shoulder, shuddering when he felt her bite down. Phoenix shouted as he came, unable to hold back.

Serenity pulled his head down to her shoulder, and not thinking twice, he bit down. His teeth weren't as sharp as hers, but they got the job done. He felt her clench tightly around him as she came. He felt the bond Nico had told him about slipping into place. It was like their souls were merging together and becoming one. Perfect, absolutely perfect. Finally everything felt right in his life.

Sighing, he pulled Serenity on top of him, snuggling her close. As he slipped into sleep, Phoenix vowed to himself that he would keep Serenity safe at all cost. She was the most important thing in his life. He was not going to lose her.

Chapter 23

Serenity woke up to a hand running up her thigh, past her waist, then cupping her breast. "I fucking love these," Phoenix growled as he lightly squeezed it before rubbing his thumb over the nipple. Serenity gasped at the sensations that flooded her body. Leaning down, Phoenix licked the nipple, nibbled lightly using his teeth, and then sucked it all the way into his mouth. When he was done with that breast, he moved on to the next one, lavishing it with just as much attention as he had the first.

"Oh God," Serenity moaned, her body shaking. Fire was igniting in her veins and she needed Phoenix in her now. "I want you, Phoenix, please," she begged, arching into his mouth.

"You know what I want?" Phoenix rasped around her nipple. Shaking her head frantically, Serenity moaned loudly. "Hush, Beauty," he whispered. "We aren't alone. Everyone else is in the kitchen eating breakfast."

Serenity's eyes widened as she remembered where they were. She tried to push his head away from her breast, but he just chuckled. "Back to what I want," he continued. "I want to taste every inch of your gorgeous body, all the way down to your delectable tiny toes. But since we don't have time for that, I'm gonna do this instead." Grabbing her by the hips he flipped her over onto her stomach. Serenity gasped as she felt his tongue tracing the phoenix tattoo on her back, starting at its head on her shoulder and moving down to the feather right above her tail bone. "You are so fucking sexy, Serenity," he groaned. "I want to kiss and lick you from top to bottom."

Phoenix slipped a hand down her back and up over her ass, sliding it around onto her stomach, he continued to move down more until he found her clit and began rubbing it. He kissed his way slowly back up to the top of the tattoo. Serenity ground against his hand until he moved and slipped two fingers inside of her. "Please, Phoenix," she begged. "I want you inside of me. I need you to claim me again."

Phoenix pulled her onto her knees and positioned himself behind her. Grabbing her hips, he pushed himself as deep as he could go inside her slick heat. Serenity loved the way they fit together, and as soon as he stopped to give her time to adjust, she started pushing back against him. She didn't want to wait. She wanted him to move now. Growling, Phoenix grabbed a fist full of her hair, pulling her head back as he quickened his thrusts.

"Tell me you're mine," he demanded as he thrust harder into her. "Yours," she panted. "I'm yours, Phoenix." Pulling her head to one side, Phoenix leaned down and bit her again on her shoulder, in the same spot he had marked the night before. She bit down on her lip to keep from screaming as he slammed harder and harder into her. Serenity's orgasm came on fast and she came, crying out his name. With one last thrust, Phoenix finished inside of her. The stayed like that for a moment trying to catch their breath. Then Phoenix slowly untangled his hand from her hair and dropped to the bed beside her, pulling her so she lay across his chest. He loved holding her like this.

Softly stroking her hair, he whispered, "I think we better have a talk, Serenity. I should have asked you some questions last night before you claimed me, but I wasn't thinking clearly. All I could think about was being balls deep in you."

Pulling back to look at him, Serenity raised her eyebrows. "What do you want to know?"

Kissing her softly, he pulled her back down in his arms and held her close. "I never asked what happens to me now that we're mated. " As she looked at him in confusion, he continued. "Do I stay human? Do I turn into a werewolf? I know you don't age very quickly. When I'm ninety, how will we be together when you still look like you're thirty? I should have asked Nico these things, but I wasn't thinking clearly."

Serenity looked at him in shock. "I have no idea, Phoenix," she told him. "We weren't allowed to mate with humans in my pack. If someone found their fated mate and they were human, our Alpha wouldn't allow them to complete the bond. He made them choose someone from our pack to mate with instead. If they refused, he killed the human."

Phoenix stared at her in confusion. "I don't understand. I thought you couldn't be with anyone else once you found your fated mate? That you were drawn to them and only them? Nico said that once he saw Jenna, that was it for him. He only gets hard for her. And personally, I can't think of anyone but you, Serenity. You consume my thoughts." Serenity blushed with pleasure at his words.

"You can as long as you haven't bonded with them, yet. So no biting, no sex. But it's hard. And they go through life feeling like a piece of them is missing. If they have already bonded, there is no way to tear them apart. The healer of my old pack tried to get me to heal a woman once because she had found her mate, but the alpha forbade them to be together because he was human. The pack couldn't figure out why she couldn't just move on and find someone more fitting. There wasn't anything wrong with her physically, which meant there wasn't anything to heal. I tried because it was expected of me, but there was nothing I could do. The enforcers ended up killing both of them. The Alpha refused to contaminate the bloodlines. He only wanted pure wolves in his pack."

"The Alpha killed two innocent people just because the man was human? And his son has been stalking you for years? What kind of fucked up pack do you come from, Serenity?"

Serenity blanched, moving out of Phoenix's arms and off the bed. This was what she had been afraid of. Phoenix finding out all of her secrets and then not wanting her anymore. But before she could get far, he was beside her and pulling her into his arms.

"Hush, Beauty," he whispered. "That was your pack, not you. You are a kind, sweet, giving woman who has been through hell and back. You're mine and there isn't anything in the world I wouldn't do for you. Don't ever feel for a minute that I think badly of you because of the way you were raised, or because of what you went through after you escaped your pack, or when you were held against your will by the General. You are one of the strongest women I know, Serenity. Own that, baby. Screw everyone else and what they think."

A sob escaped Serenity's throat as she sagged into Phoenix's arms. "I'm not strong." She insisted. "I'm scared to death, Phoenix. Scared of Malcolm somehow finding me and taking control of my mind, scared of the General's men tracking me down and taking me again, but most of all I'm scared of losing you." Once she started crying, she could not stop. She had held everything in for so long, hiding her feelings and emotions from others. But Phoenix wouldn't let her hide. She cried for the young girl she used to be, she cried for the woman she had become, and she cried for the unknown future ahead. And through the whole thing, Phoenix just held her, gently stroking her hair and whispering how much he cared for her and how special she was.

When it seemed the worst of Serenity's tears had passed, Phoenix cupped her head in his palms and tilted it up making her look directly into his eyes. "No one is ever going to take you from me, Serenity. You remember that. If it were to happen, there isn't anywhere on this earth that I couldn't find you. We've bonded. Our souls are one. And with our gifts, we will always be able to find each other."

Serenity gasped as she realized that he was right. They were one now. She would always be able to contact him if she needed him. Smiling, she whispered into his mind, *I adore you, my mate.* Phoenix kissed her, then turning her around he lightly swatted her on the butt. "Go take a shower. I'm starving." Laughing, she went to do what she was told. Phoenix loved to give orders, but she didn't mind taking them as long as they were from him.

After a quick shower, Serenity got dressed and went looking for Phoenix. She found him in the kitchen with Jenna, the children, and all of the RARE team members, along with Angel's daughter, Jade. RARE was there to come up with a plan to remove Malcolm from Serenity's life forever. But even though she was excited at the thought of being rid of Malcolm, there was a feeling of foreboding that wouldn't leave her.

Chapter 24

Angel laughed and joked with everyone around Nico and Jenna's kitchen table, but inside she was miserable. She wished she had never bitten Chase. Before it had been difficult being away from him, but now it was next to impossible. She could not eat, could not sleep. She was reunited with her daughter and she should be the happiest woman on earth. Instead, all Angel could think about was Chase and how much she missed him and wanted to be near him. Last night she had almost broken down and went to see him and the girls, Hope and Faith. She missed them, too. Having Jade back in her life didn't change how she felt about the girls. They were still hers; at least she wanted them to be. Angel had not been able to visit them in days. In her defense, she had been trying to rescue Rikki and Serenity. Hope and Faith would not understand that, though.

God, she needed Chase. This sucked. She should have run far and fast when she realized what they were to each other. Angel did not want a mate now any more than she had a month ago, but it looked like she did not have a choice. Her wolf had taken away all options when she claimed Chase as her own.

Closing her eyes, Angel took a deep breath, trying to calm down and center herself. As she did, she felt her daughter's calming presence fill her and peace spread throughout her body. All Omegas had the ability to calm others and make them feel at peace. With Jade near, Angel felt she could get through this. For now, she just had to keep away from Chase. She had to concentrate on her daughter and her work. She would do this.

The front door opened and Chase's scent enveloped her, making Angel want to grab him and finish the mate bond. Angel's mate was near and her wolf wanted him. Suddenly she heard a squeal. Turning toward the kitchen door, she had just enough time to push her chair back from the table before a little girl was launching herself into Angel's arms. Angel held on tightly until Faith started squirming to be let down. Then it was Hope's turn.

"I've missed you both so much," she told them, smiling through her tears. Hope reached up and wiped them away before leaning in and kissing her sweetly on the cheek. "We missed you, too, but Chase said you were rescuing some special people. Just like you did us. He said that we would be able to see you when you were done."

"That's right, sweetie. Rikki and Serenity were taken by some bad guys and we had to go get them back." Angel pulled both of the girls back into her arms and snuggled them close. Looking up at Chase, she smiled. But the smile was quickly wiped off her face when she saw the indifferent mask on his. Ignoring her, he walked over to the counter and started filling some plates for Faith and Hope. Angel's wolf whined and once again she felt Jade's calming presence filling her as Jade felt Angel's anxiety and tried to soothe her. Unfortunately, this time it was not helping.

"Who's this?" Jade asked with a gentle smile on her face. Jade was a kind and sweet wolf, Angel was figuring out. She had not realized Jade was an omega wolf when she was younger, but now it was obvious. Jade was sending calming vibes to everyone in the room. Unfortunately, Jade was not exactly calm herself. She was worried about Trace and was trying to deal with all of the new people in her life. Angel and Jade had spent the night getting to know one another, and Angel was very proud of the woman Jade had become. With everything she had been through, Angel was shocked that Jade was so compassionate and good natured. She could easily have become bitter and resentful.

"This is Faith and Hope," Angel told her. "I told you about them last night. My little sweethearts." Chase put the girls' plates down at the table then, without a backward glance, turned and walked out of the room.

Yep, this was definitely a craptastic moment. Settling the girls into their own seats, she stood up to follow Chase. "Girls, this is Jade, my daughter. Jade, will you please help them while I go talk with Chase?"

"Of course," Jade told her. "Go fix this." Angel nodded once and stalked out of the room. Dammit, she knew she had messed up, but this was ridiculous. Chase was going to talk to her whether he wanted to or not. She found him in the living room gazing out the window, hands clenched into fists at his sides. He did not acknowledge her presence when she walked in, so she moved to his side and stood silently trying to figure out what to say. She had messed up big time and, somehow, needed to fix it.

"Why did you bite me, Angel?" Chase ground out. "Why would you do that when we both know that you don't want or need a mate."

"I don't know," she admitted. "It just happened. When I thought about you with someone else, my wolf took over and marked you, Chase. She didn't give me a choice. I know that I screwed up, and I'm sorry. I know how hard it is for you right now, because I'm going through hell, too."

"No you don't know, Angel. You don't fucking know anything! I can't eat or sleep. I can't concentrate at work. I'm distracted when I need to handle the everyday issues in my pack. I want to tear apart everyone and everything that gets in my way right now. And to top it off," Chase shouted, "I walk around with a fucking hard-on twenty-four seven. So don't tell me that you know what I am going through, because you don't. You can't. You try taking care of two little girls like this. Oh wait, you can't because you fucking left them, too."

Angel stared at Chase in shock as he unloaded on her. She had not realized the extent that he was suffering until now. She was such a selfish bitch. She should be fixing this, but instead she was hiding from him and the situation. She was scared. She had been hurt badly before, and she would not let that happen again. There was no way she admit her fears to Chase, not that it would help if she did.

Reaching out she touched his arm, and felt his muscles bunch underneath her hand. "I'm so sorry, Chase. I don't like to see you hurting like this."

"But you don't want to be with me, either. You like your life the way it is and don't want to be bothered with a mate." Chase grabbed her by her arms and pulled her tightly against him. "Think about this, Angel. When you are home alone with no one to warm your bed. No one to share your day with. No one to love. You think about this and remember what you are missing out on."

Grabbing a hand full of her hair and holding her head in place, he slammed his lips into hers. Angel moaned as he mapped her mouth with his tongue and pushed his way inside, devouring her mouth with his. Just as quickly as it started, it ended. Pulling back Chase growled, "You remember that, Angel. No other man will ever touch you again. You are mine, whether you want to be or not. I will kill anyone who lays a hand on you."

Turning, Chase walked out of the room leaving Angel standing there wondering where her balls were. Why had she let that happen? And why had she let him stop. She was the leader of RARE, the most elite mercenary team out there. She was in charge. She made the rules. Growling, she went to find her team. They were all here for a reason, and it was time to start worrying about Serenity's predicament. Her screwed up life would have to wait.

Chapter 25

The team decided to meet in the living room while Jade took the kids outside to play. Phoenix sat down in a recliner pulling Serenity onto his lap. Nico and Jenna sat on the couch in front of them while everyone else stood against the walls.

"Where's Trace?" Phoenix asked Angel. He had not seen him at breakfast, but assumed he was coming to the meeting. It was not like him to miss something this important. Especially if it involved a member of the RARE team.

Angel moved to the center of the room. "Trace had some things to take care of. He will be gone for a couple of months. Bran is with us now, so we won't be down a team member. And soon, after her training, Flame will be joining us."

"The hell she will," Bran interrupted. "My mate is not going to be on this team."

"Yes, she is," Angel informed him. "And if you have a problem with that, you can leave. Flame has worked hard and is earning a place with RARE. If you can't watch her in action, then I suggest once she is on board, you go back to being Chase's beta."

Bran got in Angel's face, growling loudly. "It's not up to you. She is my mate, it's up to me."

"That's where you are wrong, asshole," Angel growled right back, hands clenched in anger at her sides. "And you better stand down before I put you down. Flame may be your mate, but she is not your possession. She is her own woman and can make her own decisions. She asked to join RARE, and I want her on my team. You can like it or not. I really don't give a shit. End of story."

Bran stepped towards her, but Chase let loose some of his Alpha power that had Bran backing off fast. "As soon as Flame joins your team, Bran will be back with me. He will not have a problem with it and he will not interfere."

A muscle ticking in his jaw, Bran turned and walked over to glare out the window. Phoenix watched the show in amusement, but as soon as it was over, he got down to business. "We need to look into Serenity's old pack, Angel. She and her parents ran from them years ago after they abused her gift. Not only that, but the Alpha's son, Malcolm, is a psychotic bastard that thinks Serenity is his mate and has been tracking her down since they left. They were able to stay ahead of him for a few years, but then he caught up with them and killed her parents. She unloaded a clip into him and ran, but he's still after her."

"What pack do you come from, Serenity?" Jaxson, RARE's technologist expert asked. "I can look into them and see what they have been up to since you left. I can also try and track down Malcolm."

Phoenix felt Serenity stiffen in his arms. Fear rolled off her in waves. He growled softly, surprising himself and everyone else in the room at the actual wolf sound that emerged. He had growled numerous times in his life and never once had he sounded like a real wolf. This was different. He really needed to talk to Nico about what to expect now that he was mated. Shaking his head, he cupped Serenity's chin and guided her gaze up to his. "Talk to us, Beauty," he told her. "I promise you, I will protect you. We need the information if we are going to be able to help you."

Shuddering, she nodded. Turning to Jaxson, she told him, "I was born into the Black Wolf Pack in a small town in Montana. The Alpha was Dexter Drummond; his son is Malcolm Drummond. We were a small pack because the Alpha did not believe in mating outside of our species. Everyone in our pack was to mate with a wolf. If anyone refused, they were killed. Not only could you not mate with humans, you could not mate with any other shifter that was not wolf either. No cats, no bears, nothing."

"What town was it?" Jaxson asked as he moved towards a desk in the corner. Taking out his laptop, he started setting it up. "Greenwood," Serenity told him. "The town is so small, it's probably not even on the map. It was mostly made up of my pack."

Nodding, Jaxson sat at the desk and began clicking away on the keyboard. "There's more," Serenity said nervously. "Malcolm is very powerful. He can connect with people like Angel and I can. He doesn't slip into your mind, he slams into it and takes over quickly when you are not expecting it. And...he makes people do things they would never do otherwise. He gets a kick out of watching it. Malcolm likes having total control over another person. If you get close enough, you will not be able to stop him. He will try and make you kill one another, or even kill yourself. You need to be very careful."

"How do you keep him out of your head, Serenity?" Angel asked. "I've had a lot of practice," Serenity told her. "It was harder to keep him out when I was younger, but over the years my gift has become stronger and it is easier to block him out."

"So he has done this to you before?" Angel asked. Serenity stiffened and Phoenix pulled her closer. "Yeah, he has used his abilities on Serenity," he told them. "She tried to get away from the pack once by herself before she and her parents left. When she was several miles out, he connected with her and made her come back."

Angel was watching Serenity closely. "That's not the only time, is it Serenity," she asked her softly. "He's done something else, hasn't he?" Serenity crawled out of Phoenix's lap and moved over to stand in a corner of the room, her back against the wall. She wrapped her arms tightly around her waist, bowing her head in shame. "No, that wasn't the only time," she told them. Phoenix had not realized that Malcolm had taken over her mind more than just that one time. Damn it, he should have asked.

"Talk to me, Serenity," he said to her. "What else did he do?" Serenity looked at him with eyes filled with humiliation. He was going to kill the bastard, Phoenix thought as he watched her. Malcolm was going to suffer a slow, painful death.

Serenity swallowed hard and murmured, "He used to take over my mind and try to make me think I wanted to be with him. The first time he kissed me, I let him because I thought it was what I wanted. I mean, I knew Malcolm wasn't my mate, I knew I wasn't attracted to him, but when he had a hold of my mind, I thought it was reality. I thought it was what I wanted. When he broke his hold over me and I realized what he had done, I was so ashamed. Malcolm just laughed. That's when I started working with my gift, building walls to try and keep him out. A couple of weeks after that, Malcolm connected with me again. I tried to shove him out of my mind, but he was just so strong. He had me remove my clothes and touch myself. He made me do it while thinking of him. I was so disgusted. This time I knew for sure that it wasn't me, but I had no control over it. What made it worse was that I was aware of what was happening the whole time, but I couldn't stop it. I ran for the first time after that happened. I ran because I was in constant pain from healing everyone in the pack, but I also ran because I was afraid of what Malcolm would try and make me do next. When he brought me back, he beat the hell out of me in front of the entire pack. After that my parents and I ran. We were on the run for years until he caught up with us and killed my parents. I shot him. I unloaded my gun into him. But somehow he lived. I know Malcolm's still out there. He still tries to connect with me, but he can't get in because I'm stronger now. I am never going to let that asshole mind rape me again."

A loud crack vibrated throughout the room. Phoenix looked down. Oh shit, he thought. He had broken the arm on the recliner. Raising his eyes up to Nico, he said. "I think we need to have a talk about what happens when a shifter mates with a human."

"I see that," Nico responded. "I'm not sure what to tell ya, though. I've never known a shifter that has mated with a human before. I have no clue what happens."

"I think you better have that talk with me," Chase said. "I have the answers you need."

Taking a deep breath, Phoenix nodded. "We better do it now," he told him.

"Alright," Angel said. "Jaxson you know what you need to look into. I want to know everything there is to know about that Black Wolf pack in Montana. I also want to know everything there is to know about Dexter and Malcolm Drummond. Rikki, I want you to head over to the shooting range. You will find Flame there. Give her some pointers, and then it's time to start her hand-to-hand combat training."

As Bran growled low in his throat, Angel glanced at him in disgust. "You better rethink your attitude, Bran. Flame is a strong, independent woman. She won't appreciate you trying to hold her back. She has her mind set on becoming a part of my team. If you try and tell her she can't, she's going to tell you to go get bent. Try supporting her instead of controlling her. Trust me, you will get a lot further." Bran stared silently at her, until he finally looked away in defeat.

"I would like to go with Rikki, please," Jade requested. Angel turned around in surprise, noticing Jade there for the first time. "All my life I have been defenseless. I want to learn how to take care of myself."

"But you're an omega," Angel told her. "Omega wolves are docile and peaceful. They calm the entire pack when needed. They do not fight."

"I don't care," Jade told her. "I need to know how to defend and protect myself. Omega or not, this is what I want, what I need. My mate is not here to protect me right now and you can't always be around."

"Ok," Angel relented. "You go with Rikki. After training, I need you to come back here to Jenna's and help her watch over the kids. Everyone else be at my place at 5p.m. so Jaxson can tell us what he's found and we can make plans. You are welcome there, too, Chase. The girls can stay with Jade. Rikki, make sure and bring Flame to the meeting. I want her insight."

"If you don't want to do this, I understand," Serenity interrupted. "I would never expect you to put your lives in danger for me. I don't want you to. I can find another way to get rid of Malcolm."

"Bullshit," Angel barked. "You are family. We take care of family. We will find Malcolm and eliminate the problem. And after that we will hunt the General. You are going to be free, Serenity. I've gotta go, but I will see you at my place later." With that, Angel turned and left the room.

Phoenix sat waiting patiently as everyone said their goodbyes. Serenity was still standing a distance away from the others, her arms wrapped around herself, a desolate look on her face. "Serenity," Phoenix called to her softly. When she did not respond, he raised his voice slightly. "Serenity." Slowing, she raised her eyes and finally acknowledged him. "Come here, Beauty. We need to figure out what's going to happen to me." Holding out his hand, he patiently waited for her to cross the room and slip her fingers into his. Then he tugged her down into his lap where she belonged. Pulling her close, he gently kissed her soft lips. *It's going to be ok, sweetheart,* Phoenix whispered into her mind. *Everything's going to be just fine.* Serenity snuggled into him. *I don't know what's wrong with me, Phoenix. Normally I'm a strong person, but right now I feel so weak. Why?*

Nobody can be strong all of the time, baby. But I'm here. I'll be strong for you. Nuzzling her neck, he placed soft kisses up the side to her ear. Sitting back in the chair, he pulled her closer, stroking her hair while they waited for the room to clear.

Once everyone was gone, Chase moved to the couch across from Phoenix and Serenity. Nico and Jenna sat next to him. "Congratulations, you two," he said. "I bet you are wondering what happens now, since Phoenix was human when you mated."

"Was?" Phoenix questioned.

"Yeah, your life's about to change drastically," Chase told him. "Normally your first shift takes place on the first full moon after the exchange of saliva and bodily fluids with your mate, but you will show signs of your wolf beforehand. Do you feel any different?

"Hell yeah", Phoenix said. "I feel even more protective and predatory over Serenity. I'm growling for real and things smell different. I'm also a lot stronger."

Standing up, Nico clapped Phoenix on the back. "Obviously," he said laughing as he nodded towards the broken arm of the chair. Welcome to the pack, buddy."

"Actually, that's something you need to discuss with each other. I can offer each of you a place in my pack, if you want. Nico chose to stay with Angel's pack. I understand his decision and honor it, even though Jenna is still a part of mine. Angel can keep his wolf in check, and he trusts her. Even if you choose to be with Angel, I would like to offer you a place to stay here in the compound. Originally, I was going to offer you an apartment, but Jenna called me last night and told me that you would like to keep Hunter with you. I have a two-bedroom house a mile from here that I have used for guests. I would like to offer that to the both of you. It's fully furnished, but you are welcome to make any changes you would like. It will be your home for as long as you want, and Serenity will always be under my protection here in the compound. When you leave for your missions, Phoenix, know that she will be safe."

Phoenix sat in silence for a moment thinking everything through. He was about to get his fur on probably at the next full moon, he had a new mate and cub that depended on him. His mate had two different crazy men after her. He had to decide who was going to be his Alpha. And he had to choose where to live. Well, he was going to pick the easy one to answer first. "We would like the home. My condo is no place for a bear cub and Serenity will not be safe until Malcolm and the General are dealt with."

"You got it," Chase grinned. "And you can let me know on the Alpha thing later. But you will want either Angel or I with you on your first change. It can be painful and we can help you through it."

"Angel has a lot on her plate right now. We'll call on you when it happens, Chase. Thank you."

"Not a problem. I need to get to work, but Jenna can show you to your new home. I will see you at Angel's this afternoon." Pulling out his phone to make a call, Chase walked out with a wave of his hand.

"Well I do have one question for ya, Phoenix," Nico said. "When are you going to fix my chair?" Serenity burst into laughter. The sweet sound was music to Phoenix's ears.

Chapter 26

Flame took aim and unloaded her gun at the paper target in front of her. When the last bullet left the chamber, she set the gun down on the ledge in front of her and reeled in the target. "Good shooting, Flame," she heard a voice say. Swinging around at the sound, she saw Rikki and another woman heading towards her.

"Not good enough," she responded. "As much time as I spend here, you would think I could hit the target dead on every time. But I'll get there."

"It's alright. That's what I'm here for. This is Jade, Angel's daughter. The both of you are in training today. Right now we are shooting, then it's hand to hand combat. We are to be at Angel's at 5 this afternoon for a meeting."

As Rikki talked, Flame hooked up another paper target and sent it back out. Picking up her gun and removing the clip, she loaded the bullets and slammed the clip back into place. "What's going on? Why am I in on this meeting?"

"Phoenix's mate, Serenity, needs our help. Seems the General isn't the only one after her. The Alpha's son of her old pack is stalking her. Jaxson's doing some research on it now, and we are meeting at Angel's so he can give us the dirt. Then we are going to decide how to proceed."

"And I'm in?" Flame asked excitedly. "You're in on the meeting. I can't tell you if you are in on anything else. I don't know. Bran's going to be there, too." Flame stiffened, but kept silent. "It's alright," Rikki told her. "Angel already put him in his place and Chase backed her up. When Angel is ready to bring you on, Bran will go back to being Chase's beta."

"And Bran was ok with that?" Flame asked. "I find that hard to believe. He has already made his opinion clear. Loudly. I am to stay at home and be the meek little mate while he goes out and kills all the bad guys. Screw that. That is not me. If that's what Bran wants, he can go find a new mate. I don't have time for one now anyway." Turning back around to face the target, Flame picked up her gun and quickly unloaded the clip. Lowering the gun back down, she pulled in the paper target. With a satisfied smile, she showed it to Rikki and Jade. There was a huge hole right in the middle of the bullseye.

"Perfect," Rikki grinned widely. "Looks like you just need to get a little pissed off. Oh, and for the record, Flame, Bran can't find a new mate. You are it for him. Shifters are given one true mate, a soul mate. If you reject him, he won't find another. Hell, I don't even think he can have sex with another woman now that he's found you. I could ask him, though. It's been a while since I've been with a man and Bran is fine. Maybe we could...."

Before she could finish the sentence, Flame had her down on the ground with an elbow slammed into her neck, murder in her eyes. Rikki wrapped her legs around Flame's and quickly flipped her over, holding her down. "Maybe you should think about that reaction before you so casually toss aside your mate." Jumping up, Rikki motioned for Jade to follow her and hooked another target up, sending it out for Jade to practice.

"Come on, Flame," Rikki said, not bothering to turn around. "Get off your ass and string up another target. Let's get busy. Then we will work on your takedown technique." She knew she had pissed Flame off, but she didn't really give a shit. The woman needed to wake up and see what was right in front of her before she lost it. Rikki was happy to be the one to beat some sense into her. She was looking forward to hand-to-hand combat training.

Chapter 27

Everyone was at Angel's when Phoenix and Serenity arrived. They had spent the day shopping for clothes for Serenity and Hunter and moving Phoenix's things into their new home. Chase had sent two enforcers to shadow them, which had made Phoenix feel safe enough to take his little family off compound for a couple of hours. Hunter was thrilled with his new room and excited to live with Phoenix and Serenity.

Serenity had loved every minute of the day until it came time to drop Hunter off to Jenna and Jade, at which time reality set in. She had been playing house, and now they were going to a meeting to plan out the best way to hunt down and kill a guy. Even though Malcolm had made Serenity's life a living hell for several years, actually planning a death did not sit well with her. She could kill in a do-or-die situation, but premeditated murder was wrong.

Entering Angel's home through the porch area, they walked through the kitchen and down the stairs to the basement. At the bottom of the stairs, was a room where everyone was seated around a large table. Serenity was so upset when she entered the room that she forgot to block the thoughts coming from the others. They all hit her at once.

Chase was pissed because Angel had bitten him and started the bonding process. Angel was pissed at herself for the same reason. Bran was pissed that Flame was in the room. Flame was pissed because Bran was angry that she was there. Rikki was pissed at Flame for being an idiot and rejecting her mate. Serenity could not handle it all at once. All of the anger slammed into her and she lost it. "Shut up! Everyone shut the fuck up!"

Surprised, the team turned in her direction. Phoenix put his arm around her as he looked at her in confusion. Taking a deep breath, Serenity closed her eyes and slowly built the wall in her mind, effectively blocking out everyone's thoughts.

Once she was able to function again, she walked over to the far side of the table and sat down in one of the available chairs. "Sorry about that. There was so much anger in the room, I lost control of my shields. I'm ok now."

"Anger?" Phoenix asked. "No one's angry, Serenity." Closing her eyes against a developing headache, Serenity whispered, "They are all angry with each other for different reasons. It just got to me. It was too much all at once."

"She's right," Angel ground out. "There is a lot of anger in this room. It's coming from almost all of us. With our gift, if we drop our shields, that much emotion would be painful. Get it under control, people. Jaxson, we need to focus on something else. Tell me what you got."

"I have good news and bad news. After Serenity left, to put it mildly, Malcolm went nuts. He tried to leave and look for Serenity immediately, but his dad wanted him representing the pack at some summit meeting. He told Malcolm to stand down and they would find Serenity after the pack business was handled. Malcolm killed his father in a fit of anger and took off, leaving his pack without an Alpha. One of the enforcers took over as acting Alpha until Malcolm could come back and claim the position. Malcolm never returned and the enforcer couldn't hold the pack together. The shifter council had to step in. They disbanded the pack and placed the wolves with other packs in the area. Malcolm was never found. I can't find any trace of him on my end either. He is completely off the grid."

"At least we don't have to worry about her old pack hunting her down," Phoenix said, "but why isn't there anything out there on Malcolm? It doesn't make sense. You're the best at what you do, Jaxson. If it was out there, you would have found it."

"Maybe he's living as a homeless person?" Nico responded. "Then he wouldn't have any credit cards to track, no car payments or rent."

"That's not it," Chase told them. "If he's gone off the grid, it means we are dealing with a rogue wolf. He's living primarily in his wolf form. Hunting, fishing, tracking as a wolf. And he has no alpha to keep him in line."

"Shit," Bran cursed. "If that's the case, he is going to be more dangerous than we originally thought. If he considers Serenity his mate, he will continue tracking her until he finds her, which is going to bring him here. We need to be prepared."

"So that's the plan? We just sit on our asses and wait for him to come to us?" Flame said sarcastically.

"You got a better one?" Angel asked her.

"Well, yeah. Have Serenity connect with him and find out where he is. And then we hunt him. Why sit and wait for him to get the jump on us?"

"No fucking way," Phoenix growled. "There's no fucking way Serenity is connecting with that bastard."

"It's the only way, Phoenix," Serenity said, the fear evident in her voice. "Flame's right. If we sit here and wait for Malcolm to come to us, that makes all of us vulnerable. If I can find out where he is, then we can track him."

"And what if he turns it around on you, Serenity?" Phoenix demanded. "What if he takes control of you when you connect with him?"

"That's not going to happen. I'm going to slip in undetected, get the information we need, and slip back out. He won't even know I was there. I'm strong now Phoenix. I have been perfecting my gift for years now. I can do this." Reaching out, Serenity placed a hand on Phoenix's arm, squeezing lightly. "I can do this for us, for our pack. I couldn't live with myself if someone else got hurt because of me."

"Phoenix," Flame said. "Serenity won't be going in alone. I'll go in with her. With our abilities combined, we will be strong enough to hide our presence from Malcolm."

"The fuck you will," Bran yelled. Getting up he turned and slammed a fist through the wall. Growling, he turned back to Flame and ordered, "You aren't going anywhere near that fucker's head."

"What?" Flame retorted defiantly. "You expect her to do it on her own? It's ok for her to do it, but not for anyone to be there to support her? Screw that. I'm a strong telepathic. It's one of the reasons the General wanted me."

Pacing the floor, Bran growled louder. "If both of you merge with Malcolm won't it be easier for him to tell that you are there? I don't know much about this psychic bullshit, but I would think that the more people in his head, he would be able to detect it."

"No," Flame told him. "That's not how it works. Basically, I will be piggybacking off Serenity's link. I will be there to help her hold the connection without giving away our presence and to help strengthen her gift. She will be in control."

"But you will be safe?" Bran questioned. "I have a huge problem with this Flame. I'm trying to get on board, but I don't want anything to happen to you."

"We will be fine, Bran," Flame promised. "We are strong, capable women, and we can do this. Trust me."

Swallowing hard, Bran nodded and moved to stand behind Flame, placing his back against the wall. If he could not talk her out of this crazy plan, then he would be nearby to support her.

"I still have a problem with this," Phoenix insisted. "It is my mate who is actually going into that sick bastard's mind. It is my mate who could get caught in there."

"We need to do it, Phoenix. We need to stop him before he hurts someone else. I can do this. I can track him and find him. I can beat him at his own game."

Taking a deep breath, he nodded once and leaned down to kiss her softly on the lips. "I know you can, Serenity. You are one of the strongest people I know."

Smiling at him, Serenity said, "Ok Flame, I'm ready." Flame came around to Serenity's left side, Angel moved to stand on her right. As Serenity looked up at Angel in surprise, Angel shook her head. "I am not going to let the two of you enter that asshole's mind alone. Let's do this."

Concentrating, Serenity closed her eyes and merged with Angel and Flame. She had never attempted anything like this before and was shocked at the amount of energy that flowed through her from the other women. As soon as she felt confident that she would not give herself away to Malcolm, she went hunting.

It took her several long minutes to connect with Malcolm. She had never before tried to connect with him; he was the one who always sought her out. And, she was trying to go slow enough that he didn't detect her presence. Suddenly she was inside his mind. It was a vile and hateful place, and without the added support of Angel and Flame, she would have left immediately. As Serenity sifted through Malcolm's thoughts to try and figure out where he was, she realized he was in his wolf form and was stalking prey. At first she didn't recognize the area. The land did not look familiar. But then she heard Jade's laughter. Malcolm was in the compound. Somehow he had found her and he was inside the compound.

Looking through his eyes she saw Jade pushing Lily in a swing up on a hill. Hope, Faith and Hunter were playing nearby while Jenna was laying out a snack for everyone on a blanket. As Malcolm stalked closer to Jade and Lily, Serenity screamed and broke the connection.

"Oh my God," Angel cried. "We have to get to the compound now." As she ran for the door she cried over her shoulder, "Chase, call your enforcers and send them to where that picnic area is with the swing. That area where Nico and Jenna like to take Lily. Malcolm's there! He's after Jade, Jenna and the kids." As the team raced to their vehicles, Chase placed a frantic call to his head enforcer, Slade, to fill him in.

Chapter 28

Jade was pushing Lily on the swing, laughing as Lily giggled and demanded, "Higher, higher." It was so nice to be free. With the exception of the first four years of her life, Jade had been the General's prisoner and had only seen the outdoors when she was being taken to and from the hole. Never had she seen a sky so blue, or grass so green. It was breathtaking and peaceful. She wasn't stupid enough to think she was completely safe. The General was still out there, and he was looking for her. But for now, she was happy and at peace.

Suddenly, Jade realized they were no longer alone. She felt the anger of another wolf slowly seep into her body, and knew they were all in trouble. Jade had no idea who the wolf was, but he was there for one purpose only, to kill. She had to protect the kids. Grabbing the swing, she pulled it to a stop and slipped Lily off. "Go to your mama now," she ordered pushing her towards Jenna.

"Jenna!" she screamed. "Get the kids out of here now!" Whirling around, Jade quickly changed into her wolf. Hackles raised, she growled loudly at the wolf stalking towards her. He would not get near those children. Jade was vaguely aware of Jenna and the kids were running down the hill toward the center of the compound. As the wolf tried to lunge past Jade, she bared her teeth and lunged at his shoulder. Jade had never been in a fight before, and she knew she did not have a chance in hell of winning. But she was going to do some damage and keep the wolf distracted until help go there.

Jade fought him with everything she had, but it was not enough. A few minutes later, she lay gasping on the ground. She was covered in blood from the gashes left from his teeth and claws. She also had several broken bones. The wolf had his jaws locked around her neck and all it would take was one quick jerk to end her life. She tried to send him calming vibes, but it wasn't working. He had gone wild. *Trace,* she whispered in her mind. *I am so sorry, Trace.*

Suddenly the wolf let go of her throat with a low growl, and backed away shaking its head in confusion. Growling, he dug at his ears with his paw. Jade was too weak to even raise her head, but out of the corner of her eye, she saw enforcers running up the hill towards them. The wild wolf took off, with several of the enforcers chasing him.

One of the enforcers knelt beside Jade, slowly gathering her up in his arms. She panted through the pain as tears leaked out of her eyes. "It's ok, sweet wolf," he told her. "I'm taking you to Doc Josie right now. She will fix you right up."

Jade slowly closed her eyes and let herself lose consciousness, trusting he would take care of her.

Chapter 29

The vehicles tore through the compound gates and screeched to a halt outside the hospital. Slade had been in contact with Chase and filled him in on what had happened with Jade and the other wolf. The minute the SUV stopped, Angel was out, up the hospital stairs and through the doors. Following Jade's scent, she went straight to the room where Doc Josie was examining her. Jade was still in wolf form. She was the most beautiful white wolf Angel had ever seen.

Hesitantly, Angel stroked Jade's head. She was afraid to touch her. Jade was covered in blood and it made it hard to see where she had been hurt. She slowly opened her eyes and whined softly. Then she closed her eyes, losing consciousness.

"Doc Josie, talk to me," Angel whispered. "Is my daughter going to be ok?

"She is in a lot of pain." The pack doctor told her gently. "That wolf roughed her up good. There are lacerations and broken bones all over her body, and she is so weak. He almost killed her, Angel. I honestly don't know what is holding her to us."

As tears fell down Angel's face, she felt an arm go around her waist. Leaning into her mate's chest she cried. "I just got her back, Chase. I can't lose her again."

"You are not going to lose her," Serenity promised as she walked into the room. "I'm going to save her." Moving over next to Jade's bed, Serenity gently stroked the fur around her ears.

"Thank you," Angel said on a sob. "I saw what it did to you when you healed Phoenix. You were out for days. I know how much it hurts you, but I'm not going to ask you to stop. Please, save my baby."

"I will," Serenity vowed. "I brought this hell to your door. It is because of me that Jade is lying there in so much pain. I will fix this."

Phoenix slipped his arms around Serenity, adding his strength to hers. "My mate is strong, Angel. She's proved that. I believe in her. She can do this." Serenity looked gratefully up at him, love shining in her eyes. "Let's do this Beauty."

Turning back to Jade, Serenity gently placed her hands on Jade, and, taking a deep breath, she closed her eyes. Jade's body suddenly jerked up and off the bed. Her eyes snapped open and she howled loudly. Frantically, she tried to move away from Serenity's hands, but Serenity was not letting go. It was because of her that this sweet, innocent woman was in pain in the first place. It was because of her that she lay there near death. Serenity was fixing this.

Jade howled in pain again and then passed out. Everyone in the room watched in awe as the lacerations slowly started to close. Inside Jade, her broken bones were knitting back together, causing even more pain.

Once Serenity was sure she had fixed everything she could, she slowly removed her hands from Jade, and fell back against Phoenix. "That was bad, Phoenix," she moaned as the pain took over her body. "She was so broken. I need to rest. Make sure they keep an eye out for Malcolm. He will be back. He never gives up." As Phoenix scooped her up in his arms, she whispered, "I love you, my Phoenix." With that Serenity passed out.

"Let's get her in a room," Doc Josie said. "I will make her feel as comfortable as I can right now." Moving out of the room she snapped orders to the nurses for a regular hospital room to be set up for Serenity immediately and to bring pain medicine.

As Phoenix carried Serenity past Angel, she told him, "You take care of your mate, Phoenix. I owe her. I will return the favor. When she wakes up, tell her thank you. Thank you so much." Phoenix nodded and left to take care of Serenity.

Angel looked at Jade, and as she watched, Jade slowly shifted back into her human form. Angel flinched at all the bruised and marked up flesh that was slowly healing. Walking over, she tucked a blanket up over her daughter's battered body and leaned in, placing a soft kiss on her forehead. Sitting on the side of the bed, Angel sang softly to Jade. She was aware that Chase was still in the room, but she didn't take her attention away from Jade. She had not able to be there for her the past twenty years, she was going to be here now.

An hour later, Chase got up to leave. "I have to get back to the girls. Once Jade can leave the hospital, bring her to stay at my house until Malcolm is found. She will be safe there. I will double the amount of enforcers I normally have watching Hope and Faith."

Angel turned to face him. "You are a good man, Chase Montgomery. Even though you hate me right now, you are still willing to protect my daughter. I know I have screwed everything up. My life is such a mess." Chase did not respond, just turned silently and walked out the door. Tears filled Angel's eyes as she watched him leave. Taking a deep breath, she wiped them away and turned her attention back to Jade.

Gazing down at her beautiful daughter, she whispered, "I am so proud of you, Jade. You saved Jenna and the children. You may have the soul of an Omega, but you have the heart of a warrior."

****

Jinx sat on the bed, his hands clenched tightly into fists, sweat rolling down his body. He had known the minute his sister was in trouble, and had done everything he could to help her fight the rogue wolf. Unfortunately, Jade was a smaller, weaker wolf and it had made it difficult. Finally, when Jade had been bested and almost killed, Jinx had been able to connect with the rogue wolf and make him back down. He could have done a lot more damage if the enforcers hadn't shown up. Jinx had stayed with his sister, holding her soul to earth and lending his strength to the woman who was healing her. As soon as he was sure she was going to make it, he had moved from Jade's mind to the mind of the rogue wolf. The wolf had gotten away from the enforcers, but he would not get away from Jinx. Jinx always caught his prey. And now that he knew Jade was no longer the General's prisoner, after he was done with the rogue wolf, he had bigger prey to take out. Drained of energy, Jinx leaned back against the headboard to rest and regain his strength. Then he was going hunting.

Chapter 30

Serenity was struggling to climb out of the fog she was in when she felt Phoenix's strong hand reach for her. Normally, after healing someone, it was difficult to remember anything that had happened after she lost consciousness. This time, the memories were slamming into her wicked fast. Serenity had woken up a couple of times since she had used her gift to heal Jade, and each time Phoenix had been there telling her stories of his past. Not once had she woken alone.

"So, Nico came running out of the building like someone had lit a fire under his ass," Phoenix said laughing as he continued. "You would have thought it was a pit bull as fast as he was going! Turns out a scruffy, yappy, little Chihuahua was chasing him!"

At Serenity's soft laughter, his eyes snapped to hers and he was on his feet leaning over her in an instant. "Big bad Nico was chased by an itty bitty Chihuahua, huh?" She teased hoarsely. "I've heard those things can be vicious."

Tears filling his eyes he whispered, "You're back." Turning towards the door, but refusing to let go of Serenity's hand, he yelled for the doctor. As Doc Josie ran into the room, he motioned at Serenity with a smile.

"Glad to see you are awake, Serenity," Doc Josie said with a grin. "How are you feeling? You weren't out as long this time. I'm not sure why because Jade's injuries were much worse than Phoenix's, but I think it might have something to do with the mating."

Raising the hospital bed so Serenity was sitting up, the doctor gave her some ice water. "Becca, the scientist who was rescued from the same facility you were being held in, would like to study your ability and run some tests to see why you recovered so quickly this time. Do you mind?"

Serenity stiffened at the idea of being a lab rat again. Hearing Phoenix growling as he felt her anxiety, she linked her fingers tightly with his and smiled. "It's ok, Phoenix. If it wasn't for Becca, I don't know what any of us women would have done. It is because of her that we survived. Becca hid things from the General, like my shifting. I knew I needed to let my wolf out, but I refused to in front of the General and his guards. Becca would somehow make it so the cameras would go out in my room a couple of times a month and I would shift. She also hid things for some of the other women that I am not at liberty to discuss. She was there for us, and I trust her. If she wants to study me, that's fine. As long as you are with me, Phoenix, I will be okay."

"Don't think of her as a scientist so much as a doctor. She cares," Doc Josie said. "Becca wants to find ways to help all of the women with their abilities."

"I know she does. Becca is a good person. I'm glad she was rescued with everyone else. The guards were assholes to her. They used to yell at her and beat her. Probably because she tried to protect us." Taking a sip of her water, Serenity asked, "How's Jade?"

"Jade's good, thanks to you," Doc Josie responded as she was taking Serenity's vitals. "She left yesterday with Angel. I think they are staying at Chase's until Malcolm is caught." Patting Serenity on the arm, Doc Josie told her, "And you, my dear, I would like to keep for another night. But since I know you hate hospitals, I am going to let you go home with your mate as long as you promise to take it easy the rest of the day. I still have no idea how you recovered so quickly this time, but for now I'm going to let it go and just be happy that you did."

Saying her goodbyes, the doctor left while Serenity sat in confusion trying to remember something that kept slipping her mind. She knew that there was a reason she had recovered at the rate that she had, but she could not figure it out. She also did not feel as tired as she normally did after a healing. And the pain was almost gone. "How long was I out this time, Phoenix?"

"Only two days. And you seemed like you were in more of a peaceful, healing sleep. Last time I could tell how much pain you were in. But this time, even though it was obvious that your energy was gone, you didn't seem to be in that much pain."

Serenity ran her hands down her sides, stomach and legs. "I should have been out for several days. Jade had deep cuts, bruises, and broken bones. She was almost dead, Phoenix. Shaking her head, Serenity got up out of bed, swaying on her feet a little, then walked to the bathroom. When she came back to the room, Phoenix was unpacking clothes from a duffel bag sitting on the bed.

"Can we just go home, Phoenix?" Serenity asked. "I will shower and change there. I just want to go home." Pausing, he looked up at her and grinned. "You bet, Beauty. Let's go." Shoving the clothes back into the bag, Phoenix retrieved Serenity's shoes and helped her put them on. Then, throwing the bag over his shoulder, he leaned down and scooped her up in his arms. "I can walk!" she squealed, laughing.

"Nope," he informed her. "No walking for you. The doc said rest."

"I don't think she meant that I couldn't walk, Phoenix," Serenity told him dryly. With a cocky grin, he headed out the door. "Well, then it's a good thing I make up my own rules, isn't it?"

Chapter 31

Angel had converted the old barn on her property into a workout facility for RARE. It had weights and various cardio equipment, but her favorite piece was the punching bag. It was the best way to let go of pent up aggression. As she beat the hell out of the bag, she was trying to get up the nerve to do what she knew she needed to. Angel may be RARE's badass, normally fearless leader, but sometimes things happened that scared the hell out of her. And she was not ashamed to admit that Malcolm was one of those things. Angel had seen the inside of his twisted, jacked up mind and even though she knew she had to enter it again, she did not want to. But it was important that they know where he was, and if at all possible, Angel was going to track him down and personally take him out for the pain he had caused her daughter. There was also Serenity to consider. If it was not for Serenity, Jade would be dead.

For now, Jade was safe at Chase's house resting. When Angel had left a couple of hours ago, she had not told Jade what her plan was. No one else needed to be put in danger. Grabbing the punching bag, Angel wrapped her arms around it and leaned into it. No use putting it off any longer. Waiting was not going to change the outcome.

Taking a deep breath, she turned and left the barn heading to the house. Time to shower and gear up. If she could find her balls of steel by the time the shower was done, that would be good, too.

When Angel felt like she was as prepared as she was going to be, she went to sit on the comfortable white wicker chair on the screened in back porch. Closing her eyes, she slowly drifted attempting to follow the path Serenity had taken to find Malcolm. Finally! She found him. Immediately, she noticed the dark hatred he was harboring for Phoenix. In Malcolm's mind, Phoenix had stolen his mate and that meant Phoenix must die. With Phoenix eliminated he was going to show Serenity what being Malcolm's mate was all about. She had left him and disobeyed him, but she would not make that mistake again. He would beat her into submission.

Looking out Malcolm's eyes, Angel tried to figure out where he was hiding. He was in wolf form, which she had expected, and was lying on the ground in the middle of a large wooded area. It was one she did not recognize. That night there would be a full moon. All packs like to run on the full moon, and Malcolm was planning to use it to his advantage to get him access into the compound. Once he was in the compound, he would quietly take out Phoenix. Then he was going to grab Serenity and run. Finally, he would be reunited with his mate.

Silently, Angel slipped back out of Malcolm's mind, not once noticing the other presence also lingering in Malcolm's mind. Looking out at the darkening sky, she glanced at her watch. She estimated she had no more than two hours tops before Malcolm made his move. Running outside and jumping in her jeep, Angel took off for the compound. She needed to share this information with Chase. They needed a plan and Angel needed to convince Chase not to let his pack out running tonight. One way or another, this ended with Malcolm tonight.

****

Jinx waited silently in a grouping of trees a couple of miles from the homes on the acres of land inside the compound of the White River wolf pack. He was well hidden and had taken a drug the General's scientists had invented to mask his scent, so he knew he would not be detected. It had been a simple task to infiltrate the compound for a soldier like himself. Now he just had to wait patiently for the sun to go down and the rogue wolf to make his appearance. Jinx had been born and raised for situations like this. It was child's play for someone like him. As Jinx waited, he let his mind wander, wondering about the woman he had sensed in the other wolf's mind earlier. She had seemed familiar, but not. Who was she?

Chapter 32

Hunter was spending the night at Nico and Jenna's house so that Serenity could have some peace and quiet as she recovered. She told Phoenix she was fine, but he insisted she rest because that was what Doc Josie ordered. Serenity was reclining on a wicker settee on the back porch watching the sun go down. Phoenix was sitting across from her sketching the beautiful scene. Nothing was more beautiful to him than Serenity.

As Phoenix was putting the finishing touches on his masterpiece, suddenly he cried out, dropping on the porch to all fours. He let out a loud groan as the pain intensified. "The full moon!" Serenity exclaimed. "We forgot about the full moon!" Running over to Phoenix, she grabbed his cell phone out of his back pocket and called Chase. "I'm already on my way," Chase said as he answered the phone. "Angel and I will be there in five minutes."

Hanging up the phone, Serenity knelt beside Phoenix. "Chase is on his way, Phoenix. Just a couple more minutes." Phoenix's back bowed and claws sprang from his fingertips. Throwing his head back he howled as fangs emerged from his gums. Breathing through the pain, he reached down and started undoing his jeans to strip them off. His shirt followed, then his socks. Serenity cringed as his muscles contracted painfully. Sobbing, she cried, "I'm so sorry, Phoenix."

"Not your fault," he growled, panting heavily. "Gonna be fine. Worth it to have you." Sweat covered his entire body and he was shaking with pain. "Love you so much, mate." Growling, he dug his nails into the porch, throwing his head back and howling as fur start to cover his body.

Suddenly Serenity heard a voice she had prayed she would never hear again. Malcolm stood at the edge of the porch, a cruel grin on his face. "Serenity, it is time to come home." No, this could not be happening! Before she could slam her shields back into place, Malcolm slammed into her head and ordered her to follow him.

"No, I won't do it. I won't," she moaned, grabbing her head in agony. "I am stronger now. I will not listen to you!" Squeezing her eyes shut in concentration, she threw Malcolm out of her head, quickly building the walls back up in her mind.

Suddenly there was a loud roar and Serenity was knocked to the ground as a huge dark grey wolf flew past her attacking an already shifting Malcolm. Turning to Phoenix, Serenity froze. Phoenix was gone. She quickly snapped her head back around to the battling wolves. Her Phoenix was a huge, beautiful dark grey wolf, and he was in the middle of kicking Malcolm's furry ass. The fight was a fast and bloody one, and she knew for Phoenix it was a fight to the death. Malcolm got Phoenix down on his back, but Phoenix raised his legs and dug his claws into Malcolm's soft belly, ripping it open, before throwing him off. Malcolm howled in pain, and laid there panting in misery.

At that moment, Chase and Angel ran up the stairs on the edge of the porch. Serenity felt the change in Phoenix instantly. Turning on them, he growled low and deadly, stalking towards them. "No, Phoenix," she cried out. "Stop! Malcolm is controlling you. You do not want to do this!"

Answering Phoenix's challenge with a growl of his own, Chase stripped and quickly turned into his wolf. Serenity screamed in fear as the two wolves clashed. Chase was an Alpha, Phoenix was newly turned. She had no idea how Phoenix had taken on Malcolm and won, but there was no way he would win this fight. He was already weakening. And if you made the mistake of challenging an Alpha, it was almost always to the death. The fight was quick, brutal and ended with Phoenix on the ground and Chase's teeth around his throat.

Chase quickly changed back to his human form. Serenity ran to Phoenix, his body limp. Serenity ran to him as Chase quickly changed back to his human form. Phoenix slowly shifted back to human form, but remained unconscious. "What happened?" Serenity asked Chase. "Is he going to be okay?"

"Yeah," Chase answered. "He's fine. Just drained. Most wolves don't get into two different fights immediately following their first change. He just needs rest. Where's Malcolm?"

Serenity looked around in surprise. Not only was Malcolm gone, so was Angel. Her gaze swinging back to Chase's in terror she whispered, "Angel's gone after him."

Chase nodded, sighing deeply in resignation as he pulled on his clothes. "My money is on her. Let's get Phoenix into bed. I will stay here until I know for sure you are safe from Malcolm."

Chapter 33

Angel chased after Malcolm, a throwing star in each hand. He had shifted quickly back to his human form while Chase and Phoenix were fighting, before taking off into the woods, his arms wrapped around his mutilated stomach. Angel had her mental shields in place and had to concentrate on keeping them there. She could feel Malcolm trying to break through her walls, but that was not going to happen. Malcolm was slowly pulling away from her, but Angel did not want to take the time to shift. The son of a bitch was strong and fast.

Surprising the hell out of Angel, a man dropped from the trees in front of Malcolm. Angel skidded to a stop, and as she watched, Malcolm tripped and fell on his knees in front of the stranger. "You made a big mistake when you hurt my sister," she heard the stranger tell Malcolm as he slid a long sword from a scabbard on his back. Chuckling he said, "Don't bother trying the mind games with me. I am stronger than you will ever dream of being." Holding the sword up, the man let his fangs drop as he growled, "This is for Jade." With one clean swipe Malcolm's head was severed from his shoulders.

Angel stood there in shock, afraid to believe what she was seeing. As the man looked up at her through eyes identical to Jade's, Angel let out a gasp. "They told me you were dead." Slowly she walked towards him as tears streamed down her face. "All these years, I thought you were dead."

Narrowing his eyes he asked, "Who are you?" On a sob, Angel stopped right before him, slowly reaching out a hand and touching his face. She pulled back quickly when he flinched and growled lowly. "I'm Jade's mother," she told him. "Your mother."

Ignoring her claim, he kneeled down, used Malcolm's clothes to clean the blood off his sword, and sheathed it in the scabbard on his back. "I have to go. Take care of Jade for me. I won't be able to for a while." Turning, he moved swiftly into the darkness.

"Wait," Angel called out. She could hear the enforcers moving towards them quickly, but she did not want to let her son go. "What's your name? How can I find you?"

Sobbing she ran in the direction he had gone. "Please, don't leave me. Please, my son." Stopping, she fell to her knees and howled in pain. She had found out after twenty-four years of thinking her son was dead, he was really alive. That someone had taken him from her. And now he was gone again. She did not know anything about him; had no idea how to find him. The pain in her heart was almost unbearable.

She felt soft words enter her mind. *I have to go before the General realizes I'm gone. I go by Jinx. When it is safe, I will find you. Take care of Jade.* He was gone as swiftly as he had appeared.

The General. That crazy motherfucker had not only stolen her daughter, but also her son. She was going to kill him slowly and painfully. Angel rose to her feet and turned back in the direction of Malcolm's body. She had to make things right in the compound first, then she was going to find the General and make him wish to hell he had never met her or her children.

When she reached where they had left Malcolm's body, several enforcers were looking from the body to his head lying on the ground several feet away. "Take both the body and the head back and burn them," she ordered. "Get the fire as hot as you can. I want to know for a fact that he is gone."

Quickly, the enforcers gathered up the remains and moved out, Angel following. She went straight to Phoenix and Serenity's home to check on them, sighing in relief when she found Chase had kept Phoenix alive. She did not think he would kill Phoenix, but sometimes Alphas could not control their wolf, especially when they were challenged. Alpha's had to prove their dominance, and in the heat of the moment, fighting to the death seemed like the only way. Standing in Phoenix and Serenity's bedroom, Angel listened as Chase and Serenity recapped what had happened after she went after Malcolm.

"What happened out there?" Chase asked her. "I was told Malcolm was decapitated." Serenity's head swung around in surprise.

It was Angel's turn to share what had happened on her end. "It wasn't me," Angel informed them. "It was my son, Jinx. God, for twenty-four years I thought he was dead. They told me he was born dead. But he was here tonight." Angel's eyes filled with tears as she collapsed in the chair by Phoenix's bed. "He had this magnificent sword. Malcolm tried to control his mind, but Jinx was so strong. He laughed at Malcolm. Told him that he shouldn't have hurt his sister, and then struck him with his sword."

Lifting her head, she looked to Chase and Serenity. "He looks just like his father except he has Jade's eyes. They are twins, but look so different. He said he had to get back before the General found out he was missing." Slamming her fist on the side of the bed, Angel snarled, "The General stole both of my children from me. I'm going to gut the bastard."

"And we are going to help you," Phoenix croaked. Serenity was at Phoenix's side in an instant. He laughed softly, holding out a hand to her. "I'm ok, Beauty. Just some minor bruises that you can kiss away later." Grinning, he turned back to Angel. "Congratulations on finding your son, Angel."

"Oh my God," Serenity exclaimed as she realized what had been escaping her consciousness since awaking after healing Jade. "It was Jinx. He is the reason I recovered so quickly when Jade was hurt. I remember a strong presence held her to us and lent me his strength when I was healing her. I didn't have to use all of my own. He was so strong. I forgot all about that until now. How could I forget that? It had to have been Jinx."

Smiling through her tears, Angel whispered, "Probably because he wanted you to." Standing up she told them, "I need to get home to my girls. I need to tell Jade about her brother. I will see all of you tomorrow. Take care Phoenix." Chase said his goodbyes and quietly followed her out of the house.

Hope and Faith were asleep when they returned back to Chase's house, but Jade was waiting up for them. Tears filled her eyes as she watched them walking up the sidewalk. Rushing forward, she threw herself into Angel's arms. "I was afraid Malcolm would hurt you." Angel pulled back smiling at her. Aware that Chase had moved on into the house to give them privacy, she responded, "He didn't get a chance. Your brother took care of him first."

"Jinx was here?" Jade asked, then slammed her hand over her mouth, her eyes widening. Stepping back she turned and quickly walked up the stairs and into the house. Angel followed slowly trying to get her thoughts in order. Jade had known about Jinx and hadn't told her? Why would she do that? A part of Angel felt betrayed by her own daughter.

Angel found Jade in the living room sitting on the sofa, her head hung down in shame. Sitting beside her, Angel clutched her hands together in her lap, took a deep breath and asked, "You knew about Jinx?"

Raising her eyes to Angel's, Jade whispered, "Yes, I did. The General brought him to see me when I was first taken. We were so young, but he was already training to be a soldier. We talk sometimes, but no one knows. The general uses me to make Jinx do whatever he wants. Jinx is a good person, but he does horrible things to protect me. I'm sorry I didn't say anything to you, but Jinx didn't want anyone to know we talk."

Closing her eyes and taking a deep breath, Angel nodded. "I understand. You were just trying to protect your brother."

"We talked about you," Jade told her. "It's how I remembered so many things from when I was younger. I told Jinx how you would read stories to me, and sing to me every night when you put me to bed. The General told him you were dead, so at first Jinx didn't believe me when I talked about you. Then he wondered why you gave him up? I told him you wouldn't have done that."

"I didn't," Angel promised her. "The doctors told me he was stillborn. I believed them. I shouldn't have, but I did. Believe me, if I had known he was out there, I would have been looking for him just like I have been looking for you the past twenty years."

Hugging Angel, Jade whispered, "I know. I remember at first you talked to me, but then I couldn't hear you anymore. I found out when I was older they have a drug that makes it so you can't telepathically connect with others and they were experimenting on me. I was never able to find Jinx, but he is so strong, he always made the connection on his end."

Leaning back against the sofa, Jade clung to Angel's hand. "I'm scared. The General doesn't have me anymore. That means he has nothing to hold over Jinx's head."

"Jinx is going to try and take him down, isn't he?" Angel asked. "He always said when I was free a hell like nothing he had ever seen was going to rain down on the General." Jade informed her. "He isn't going to just try to, he is going to take him out."

"We can help him, Jade. We have the same ultimate goal. We need someone on the inside, he needs us. He can't do it alone. The next time he contacts you, you tell him RARE will be ready when he needs us." Standing, Angel leaned over and hugged her. "I'm going home, Jade. I need to wrap my head around all of this." Jade immediately stood up and followed her to the door.

"I'm going with you," Jade said shutting the door behind them. Slipping her hand in Angel's, together they walked to Angel's vehicle. "Family sticks together, right?"

"Yeah, baby girl, they do," Angel responded with a grin. "Let's go home."

Chapter 34

Phoenix woke up to a hand trailing down the center of his chest, over his abs, and lower still until it wrapped around his hard cock. He moaned in pleasure. Nothing like waking up with wood and having the woman you love next to you, craving the same thing you are. He jacked his hips up when he felt soft, full lips wrap around the tip of his dick and a tongue flick out. "Fuck," he groaned. Serenity laughed, which made his dick throb. Her long hair tickled his balls and he knew he was not going to last long. Grabbing a handful of Serenity's hair, he held her still while he arched into her mouth driving them both crazy.

Phoenix could not wait any longer. Growling, he yanked her up on top of him and pushed inside her in one long, deep thrust. Grabbing hold of her hips, he set a fast pace. Phoenix felt Serenity's inner muscles tighten around him and sinking her teeth into him she came. Feeling his own fangs drop, he bit deep as he shot inside her. And then, once again, everything was right in his world. Licking his bite on her shoulder, he whispered, "I love you, Beauty."

Pulling back, she graced him with a beautiful smile. "I love you, too, Phoenix." Wrapping his arms around her, Phoenix leaned down and breathed in her scent, sighing in satisfaction. The blend of both of their scents mixed together was intoxicating.

Phoenix did not know what their future would bring, but he did know that they were going to face it together. They still had some decisions to make, the biggest one being whom they were going to call Alpha, but for now he was going to concentrate on his mate. Grinning, he kissed Serenity and hopped out of bed. Turning around, he scooped her up in his arms, and throwing her over his shoulder he headed for the shower. Chuckling as she smacked him on the ass, he told her, "Let's shower, Beauty, and then go get our boy."

CPSIA information can be obtained
at www.ICGtesting.com
Printed in the USA
LVHW012251070119
603102LV00018B/789/P